The Conception of Us

Labels & Lace

YD La Mar

This is a work of fiction. Names, characters, places, and incidents either are the product of the author's imagination or are used fictitiously. Any resemblance to actual persons, living or dead, events, or locales is entirely coincidental.

First paperback edition October 2021

Book Cover: YD La Mar
Editor: Rachelle Anne Wright, Patrice "Tree" Miller

Acknowledgments

To my wonderful husband, who never bats an eye when I come up with crazy ideas, but instead just adds to it, making my stories come alive. My children, who tell me every day that they are proud of me.

To my beta readers. You guys are the real MVP. Thank you for sticking with me through the initial phases of my writing journey. All of your feedback has inspired me to better myself and my writing ability. Anita, Alex, Dana, Vicky, Maria, **Tree**, Beth, Shaddy, **Kylie**, Gloria, Sasha, and **everyone** who responded to my beta request in the dark group, and everyone else who beta read, thank you for bouncing ideas with me.

To all my readers, thank you for giving me the chance. I hope I can continue to make you guys proud.

Blurb

How did a 28 year old virgin like myself catch a woman like her?
From the first time I saw her behind the camera lens, I knew she was out of my league.
Every man's fantasies come to life, I couldn't get her out of my mind.
Out of all the guys she could have, she chose me, the nerdy Malay guy.
I'm so nervous about bringing her to meet my family, my palms are sweating.
What if they're too much for her?
What if I'm not enough for her?
What if she decides she can't handle the fact that we can't do anything before marriage?

Catching her isn't going to be enough.
The hard part is finding a way to keep her.

Courtesy Warning: This book may contain triggers for some. Triggers include but not limited to: light BDSM

Names & Families

Mohd Akmal Bin Alqi

Veronica "Vero" Hernandez

Nora - Akmal's mom

Rafil - Akmal's dad

Hasanah

Sakinah

Hidaya

Auntie Irina

Uncle Tuah

Cousin Ismail

Cousin Aryani

Auntie Adila

Uncle Zaka

Cousin Umar

Cousin Nosiah

Fabian Hernandez

Maria Hernandez

Alejandro Hernandez

Matunaagd Big Crow

Atsuko Kobayashi

Bisaam

Translations

MALAY

Makan, Makan - Eat, Eat

Don't be perasan la - don't flatter yourself (la is sometimes added at the end of sentences)

Ibu, don't kacau him - mom, don't disturb him

Walao eh - Oh my god/oh shit

Can hah - Are you sure?

Bapa - dad

Ibu - mom

Cantik - beautiful/pretty

SPANISH

¿Mira, mira quien viene? - Look, look who's coming

Milagro que se acuerda que tiene familia - It's a miracle that she remembers she has family.

La bendición - asking for blessing, typical greeting

Que Dios te bendiga - God bless you, reply to La bendición

Comida - food

¿Quién es tu amigo? - Who is your friend?

¿Porque? - Why

por una semana - for one week

Tu papá estaba preocupado - your dad was worried

Mira tu boca! - Watch your mouth

¿Quién es tu novio? - who is your boyfriend?

ven a hablar conmigo por favor - come talk to me please

Siéntate por favor - sit please

Esposo - husband

Explícamelo - explain it to me

Es un buen chico - He's a good boy

un buen chico puertorriqueño - a good Puerto Rican boy

Hija - daughter

¿Estás embarazada? - you're pregnant?

Vamos, antes tu papá y hermano... - Come on, before your dad and your brother...

Seria/serio - serious

Silencio - be quiet

Dramatica - dramatic

Buen provecho - enjoy your meal

Mira mi culo - Look at my ass

Pero - but

Pinche - fucking..

Dios Mio - My god

Author's Forward Note

Book 2 is starting off right where we left off with book 1. In fact, *The epilogue of book 1 was told from Akmal's perspective. Chapter 1 of this book will be the same moment from Vero's perspective.*

Recap: Mat and Atsuko are engaged. Vero has been hanging out with Akmal and has now ended up under his wing and living inside his home, because he didn't like the idea of her living alone next to a bunch of frat boys. Akmal's culture dictates that though he is allowed to date, he isn't allowed...those kinds of touches until marriage.

Now that the stage is set for a wedding ceremony (Akmal's mother is probably already setting it up before Vero even gets there), can you imagine loud-mouth, overconfident Vero having to restrain her inner self when the wedding happens? I was informed that this would actually be a WHOLE DAY affair. She would have to refrain from cursing as well.

I hope you guys are excited to see what book 2 has in store for us all! These characters take over my story as I write. I don't even know what's going to happen next!

> ***This book contains authentic speech used by the different nationalities/ethnicities represented in this book. Some grammar was purposely done with broken English to continue to allow the story to flow authentically.***

Tree & Kylie, this one's for you gals.

Chapter One

VERO

Akmal is driving us home and I'm still thinking about the plan I concocted at Atsuko's place. I need to get his inhibitions down so that I can convince him to let me touch him. He's so hands-off that it drives me nuts. I'm not used to working this hard, but it brings out my competitiveness. Does that make me a bad person? I don't think so since I've been trying to be good since I met the bastard.

Okay, he's really not a bastard but I'm so damn horny I can't think straight right now. His culture is making it difficult for me to get close to him. He's mentioned that they do date but I can't even touch the guy without him backing away from me. I'm going to have to take this into my own hands or else I'll die from sexual frustration.

Akmal walks us towards *our* door. Can you believe it? I felt like I deserved a gold medal for somehow convincing the guy to let me in his damn door. It's dark out and my mind comes up with a plan before he can escape me and retreat back to his room like he always does.

"Akmal, do you want to watch a movie with me?" Uh-oh, he looks unsure. I cant my hips a little to the side as I cross my arms over my chest, pushing the girls up a bit. His eyes flick quickly there and away. *Sneaky, sneaky boy.*

"Yeah, what do you feel like watching?"

"Whatever you want. I'll go grab us some drinks." *Come on baby, trust me. I'll take care of you tonight. You won't regret it.*

I don't know what Akmal is putting on the big screen in the living room and I really don't care. At this point, my mind is on the mission. Shooting lots of smiles his way, I pass him bottle after bottle. I can see after two, he's getting a little tipsy. *This is going to be fun. I knew Akmal was a lightweight.*

We start watching Star Wars Episode 1, and three quarters into the movie, my mouth is watering at the sight of his crotch. *I'm finally going to meet you today, baby. You and I are going to kiss and make up for the time lost.*

Akmal's eyes are slowly drifting closed and I stare at his gorgeous face. He's so different from any of the men I've been with. My thumb caresses his cheekbones as the palm of my hands cradles his face. How can this man make me lose myself when I've barely even gotten anything in return?

I feel like any scrap of attention he gives me makes my damn world shine brighter and I've already become addicted to it. Addicted to him. Addicted to the one person I can't seem to catch and I am too much of a selfish ho to let anyone else have what I've claimed as mine. Climbing over him, my determination burns inside of me as my breasts rub against his shirt.

There's always something between us. Why is that? And what is holding him back from me? Am I not good enough to love? I mean, plenty of men come up to me and proposition me, so how can that be? Sure, they're probably all in it for their benefit but I'm not that bad, right? After meeting Akmal that day at the car show, I couldn't put myself out there for a quick fix anymore. Not when there's a prize dangling in front of me in challenge.

I've broken at least two vibrators already and I'm too damn stubborn to get another one. I've been borrowing Atsuko's dildo. I'm sure she doesn't mind since she gets to jump on Mat's cock whenever she likes now.

But how about me? I want a cock to call my own. I mean, I never thought I'd see the day but after witnessing what Atsuko has with Mat, I can't help but feel a pang of emptiness in my gut. Was that what I've always been missing and just didn't know it?

My hand slides down Akmal's warm chest as I watch his breathing slow. The gentle rise and fall creates a soothing lullaby to my senses. He's always had a calming presence about him and it's heady. It makes me want to soak it all up, crawl into him, and just let all my fears go.

My fear is that a man as perfect as Akmal would never want a girl like me. I'm probably not good enough but it doesn't stop me from wanting him all the same.

Determination spurring me on again, my hands deftly start to undo the obstacle before me. My mouth is watering again. I just want to make him feel good, show him I can make it all about him and that I'm not as selfish as I might seem before his eyes. I can be good.

Gosh, just his thigh between my legs is stoking the fire that's already going. A moan slips out of my lips. That damn dildo didn't help one bit.

"Vero?" His voice is doing something to me. Would this be what he sounds like waking up? The hole in my gut is turning into feelings of yearning. The last guy I woke up to was my high school sweetheart. The day he threw my heart away after he got what he wanted from me.

"Shh...let me take care of you." He doesn't notice me caressing his cock in my hand as I take it out of his pants. He's circumcised and the head is staring at me and winking. I think it wants to come out and play. "It looks angry."

Letting out a breath across his tip, I can feel his dick getting harder in my hand. *My god, Akmal.* How has he been hiding this? I take that back. He needs to be hiding this because I'm about to swallow it fucking whole.

When his taste hits my tongue, my mind gets lost in lust. Has anything felt so good in my mouth before? Akmal feels so forbidden that my pussy is clenching at the fact that I've finally caught him in my clutches. Shit, I want to worship this cock, he tastes so good. My tongue swirls around the head of his cock like it's a dessert I can't get enough of.

His moans do something to me. He's still trying to hold it back but the booze is making his inhibitions go down. No time feeling bad about that right now when I'm grinding my pussy onto his lower leg.

He moans again louder and I feel proud, I feel like I'm in competition with myself as my tongue continues to explore and dance across his slit. Baby boy precums again and now it's my turn to moan with his cock in my mouth. When I lift my sights to him, he's staring right back at me with hooded eyes. *That's it, I want you to let go and let me take care of you.*

I'm hot. I'm horny. I want this man to cum in my mouth and give me all he's got. I suck harder as my hands drift down to fondle his sack and that must have been the magic touch because Akmal starts to pulsate into my mouth, inadvertently making me take him in deeper, almost gagging.

My god.

That is so sexy.

Yes. Give it all to me.

After swallowing every last drop, I moan again, giving him one last lick across the top.

The serene look on his face makes me smile as I climb over him, making sure to drag my pussy along for some friction. Can anyone blame a girl? Look at this man.

Akmal slowly reaches out to me and it makes me fucking shine. *He's finally reaching for me.* When he cradles my face, I feel like offering my heart to him on a silver platter. The way his eyes bore into mine like I'm the only one he sees. Has any man ever looked at me this way? My heart secretly breaks a little when my mind mentally answers me with a solid no.

Putting on a good front, I give Akmal a smile because he genuinely does make me happy. I wake up thinking about him and go to sleep thinking about him.

"Hi." He looks vulnerable. I wonder what he's thinking. I wonder what he thinks of me now?

"Will you be my wife?" Holy shit, I did not see that coming. The butterflies are having riots in my stomach. I'm not one to be held down because I don't want my heart to be trampled on by fuckboys. But Akmal...*Oh, Akmal.* Fuck it, if I don't scoop him up some other ho will, I just know it. That thought makes me want to shank a ho. Hells no. This fool is *my prize.*

"Damn, if all it took was a blowjob to make you see me, I would have done it sooner. Fuck it. Why not? Hell yeah, I'll be your wife."

His eyes are so open, so vulnerable. I feel my heart swell and seal the potential for hurt with a kiss. Akmal is too good of a man to hurt me, right? You only live once and if this is where I had to choose, I'd choose him every time.

He doesn't seem like he knows what he's doing, but that's okay. He better strap up because I plan to give him the ride of his life.

Chapter Two

VERO

The booze made Akmal more open to persuasion but I didn't want to scare him off. Our kisses became hot, heavy and really wet. I must have been tired too because I wake up on top of a pretty lumpy bed.

When the bed lets out a masculine groan, my girl parts wake up with excitement.

"Good morning, Akmal." Giving him a peck on the cheek, I'm taken by surprise when he startles, jumps and inadvertently throws me off the couch onto the floor.

Oomph.

At least I landed on my ass, and good thing I got some junk in my trunk to soften the fall. Damn that kind of hurt.

There's the sound of scrambling and suddenly Akmal falls right on top of me, knocking my head back onto the floor. *Ahh fuck it.* I'm just going to lay here for a second as the little birdies fly around my head.

"Shit, I'm so sorry, Vero. Y-y-you surprised me." He's scrambling to remove his body from laying on top of mine but is only succeeding in pushing my tits every now and again before his hands find solid ground.

I laugh, because what the hell am I supposed to do? The morning wood pressed against my core is making me a little light-headed too.

"Akmal, if you wanted to grope me, all you had to do was ask. I love tit play." My hands reach out to grab the front of his shirt to bring him a little closer to me.

"Shit." He jumps off me like I got the plague and plants his ass on the couch while rubbing his hands down his face.

By the time I bring myself up to sit next to him, he's leaning forward with his head in his hands and his elbows on his knees. The groan he lets out makes me wince a little. Poor guy must have a hangover. Sorry, not sorry.

Rubbing the back of his shoulder, Akmal almost stumbles off the couch again when he jumps to the far end of the couch. What is up with this guy? I'm starting to get a little grumpy with how he's treating me right now. Rude.

He rubs his face with his hand one more time and pulls his hair a bit.

"Vero, we-we can't touch like that before marriage. My culture doesn't allow it. Fuck, my culture doesn't allow drinking, and last night was a lapse in judgment." Oh, hell no. I'm about to fucking leave this damn apartment when his hand shoots out to tentatively touch the top of mine.

"Vero, please listen to me. I meant what I said last night. I want to be with you. You don't know how bad I want to be with you. You drive me crazy. The only way I *can* be with you, is this way. Please understand." The tension in my body leaves me at that admission.

There are those vulnerable eyes again. I never realized his culture was that restrictive. Now I feel a little worse for what I did to him last night. But if I didn't do that, would we really be here right now talking about finally being together? Am I really fucking doing this?

My eyes sweep over Akmal's tousled hair, sincere face, and apprehensive eyes. Is he...is he scared of me changing my mind about last night? My goodness, *this poor baby*.

I must come off like that kind of girl. What a slap in the face that thought is, a slap I probably needed.

"If that's the way it has to be, I'll try it. I don't know what I'm up against here, Akmal. You're going to have to hold my hand the whole way, okay? You can trust me. I'm going to do my best. For you."

It's at that very moment that Akmal's eyes shift to my lips. What the hell, man? You can't tell a girl she needs to put on a damn chastity belt and then look at me like you want another taste. *Naughty, naughty Akmal.*

AKMAL

My palms are sweating. I've dropped my phone three times already and Vero isn't helping. At least she finally stopped walking in front of me, but now she's sitting there in the smallest shorts known to man and a tank top. Her nipples are popping out against her shirt and it's making me sweat. How am I supposed to concentrate on what I need to do?

Maybe this is a bad -

The ringing against my ear stops.

"Hello? Akmal? Are you calling because you want to bring a girl home? Do I need to get things ready?"

"Ibu, geez. I'm just calling to let you know I'll be dropping by tomorrow."

"That's it? Aye, okay but are you bringing Mat? Bring Mat. I'll let Hasanah know he's coming. There will be plenty to eat. See you tomorrow, eh?"

She hangs up on me and I let out a long breath. Damn, that was nerve wracking. It shouldn't be, since I'll actually be bringing someone this time.

"You're leaving me tomorrow, Akmal?" She has an accusing tone and it's making me feel guilty.

"What? No!"

"You didn't tell your mom I was coming. Won't she be upset?"

How do I explain to this beautiful woman that my mother would have probably prepared the wedding before she even knew her correct dress size? I want Vero to have a chance, a chance to make sure she's making the right decision. I really hope she still wants to marry me after meeting the family. I'm cringing on the inside at the thought of tomorrow.

"Vero, it's - it's complicated. My mother can be a bit over-bearing. I wanted you to get a chance to get to know what you're walking into before ... before..."

"Before what? Is there something I need to know about? Do you have a girlfriend in the wing or something? A lover waiting for you?"

"What? No! No, no - nothing like that. Sheesh, Vero. I'm not that kind of guy."

"Then tell me, what are you afraid of? What are you afraid of me finding out about?" She shifts her legs and my mind goes blank for a second. My goodness, her legs. Now I'm getting lightheaded since all my blood has rushed down between my legs.

I let out an exasperated breath because this is exactly why I've been single for twenty-eight years. How do people even deal with this kind of pressure? My head is about to explode. From my mother and now Vero.

Running my hands down my face, I try to find the right words to let her know what I'm thinking.

"I-I'm not good at this. Vero, please believe me. I just don't want you to have any doubts about what you're walking into. My culture is - is different. I don't want you to feel tied down because of me and I'm really hoping you'll still want me by the end of tomorrow." She's nodding slowly at my admission but also looks somewhat skeptical about what I'm saying.

Did that sound as pathetic coming out of my mouth as I feel right about now? But dammit, I want her to see me, all of me, and still want *me*. I sneak a glance at her again while my chin is in my hands and my chest constricts. She's so fucking beautiful and perfect, how could she want someone like me? Someone with no experience in anything woman related. I'm praying tomorrow doesn't end in a disaster. I already feel the heartburn from the thought of her rejection after my mom bombards her with whatever she might have planned.

Leaning forward to rub my hair again, my heart continues to burn beyond comfortable levels. This is going to be a disaster, I just know it.

Chapter Three

AKMAL

I think my cock is going to fall off with how hard it's been since that night. The moment that changed my life forever.

Today is the day. The day I finally bring a woman home to my family. Standing under the showerhead, letting the water spray down my hair, I'm staring at my angry cock. How am I going to get through a meeting with my family like this? The warm water on my skin reminds me of her mouth on my cock and I groan. Washing my body quickly under cold water this time, I step out of the shower stall and almost slip, if it wasn't for my arms grabbing onto something solid.

Vero is standing there with a towel wrapped around her body and my cock is stirring to life again. Shit. I stumble as I grab the towel off the rack and cover my crotch. I can feel my face heat up despite just having a cold shower as Vero sends a smile my way.

“Wh-wh-what are you doing here?”

“Am I not allowed to shower to get ready? I want to smell my best when seeing your family Akmal.” Shit, she’s right. Okay. I’m overthinking things. She was just waiting for me to be done.

Sidestepping while holding the towel over my crotch, my hip runs into the side of the door as I try to open it without dropping the towel. Is it the steam in the room that’s making me sweat? My mind tells me there’s a tattoo on Vero’s right arm that I never noticed before. Chancing a glance back before exiting completely I get a sight of her luscious ass - her very naked, luscious ass as she steps into the shower.

Tripping out the door, I slam it shut and run to my room to get dressed. I need to survive today and hopefully marry this woman ASAP because I don’t know how much longer I can hold out like this, living with a siren.

Standing up after I finish tying my last shoe, my heart stutters at the sight before me. Vero is leaning against the doorframe of my room only wrapped in a towel once again, hair dripping wet. This must be the smallest towel I own because it is giving me a glimpse of heaven right now and my mouth feels dry.

“Akmal, you’re going to have to help me with a dress selection because I don’t want to offend your parents.” Oh right. She’s right. Yeah, that makes sense. I don’t understand the smile she gives me before she turns and sashays towards the guest room. Shit, I need to tell her not to mention her staying here to my parents.

I'm jogging to catch up with her, speaking as I turn the corner out of my doorway. "Vero, I need to talk to you about something. When we get there don't tell anyone we -" A groan escapes my lips when she bends over to inspect some dresses laying on the bed.

The angle she's bending from where I'm standing gives me the barest of hints to a treasure I'm too damn curious to uncover. I need to fucking marry this woman quickly, before I go out of my damn mind. All my blood has rushed to my cock even more and I have to take a deep breath in and out before speaking.

Will it always be like this between us?

I don't know when I closed my eyes, but when they open back up I see Vero's face turned to look at me over her shoulder, still bent over. *My god.*

Clearing my throat, I close my eyes and try to remember what I wanted to say.

"V-Vero. When we see my family, p-please don't mention us living together. I wasn't supposed to have a woman under the same roof but you were a special circumstance."

"A special circumstance? What is that supposed to mean?" Crap, why does she sound like that? I didn't say anything wrong, did I? Opening my eyes, I see her standing there like a vixen with her hands on her hips.

That shouldn't look so sexy. She's mad, right? When girls put their hands on their hips they're usually mad. I think?

"I'm not a damn charity case, Akmal." Shit. Shit shit shit.

"No! N-n-no, that's not what I meant! Please. Crap. Let me rephrase that." One of her eyebrows lifts up but her hands haven't gone down yet. Shit.

Running a hand down my face, I take another deep breath. I need to fix this. It can't fail before it even starts.

"Vero, please. I don't regret anything. You're not a charity case, that's not what I meant. If I could do it over again, I'd do everything in the exact same way. You belong here, Vero, with me. Just the thought of you next to those animals makes my chest burn." Shit, I didn't mean to say that much, but I was on a roll. It sounded right in my head.

Her arm slowly lowers and I let out another breath only for it to hitch again when she starts walking towards me. My palms are sweaty but I don't want to rub them on my pants. When her chest is pressed up against me, Vero lifts her gaze to mine and wears an expression I can't decipher.

"Akmal, you know just what to say to make a girl feel good." My god, her voice is purring and I'm losing brain cells by the minute as my blood rushes to my cock yet again. My eyes flick to the clock on the wall. Do I have enough time for another cold shower?

Her warm hands grab my face and pull me down. We shouldn't do this. I shouldn't be this close to her when I can barely contain myself around her. I need this wedding to happen soon. I need my family to not mess anything up. My mind is racing with conversations I need to have with family members, when her lips brush mine without actually pressing them to mine.

When she speaks, her lips only whisper against my own, sending tremors down my body. How does she affect me like this? She's bringing me to my damn knees and we haven't done anything more than what's already been done.

"Akmal, breathe. Everything will be okay." Closing my eyes, I do as she says. I can feel her rub the tip of her nose against mine and my mind starts to calm. She's right. Everything will be okay. She agreed to marry me. That means she feels enough for me to go through it. It's a good start. I need to just make sure it keeps going well to keep her by my side.

When her hands leave my face, I almost protest the loss of her warmth. Shit, Akmal, keep it together man. You need to make sure she marries you. Keep to the plan.

"So what dress should I wear? I pulled out my most...conservative choices." It's almost a crime to have to cover up all that beauty, but she's right. Best to cover up a bit on a first impression.

"Um, whichever covers you up the most."

"Are you saying you don't like the way I look?" Shit.

"No! No, that's not what I meant." My hands are getting clammy again as Vero chuckles. Where am I going wrong here? Is she playing with me?

"Akmal, you are too cute. I'm only kidding. I understand. I'll make sure to make myself presentable for your family. You can trust me." Her fingertips skate across mine only for a second before she turns and bends over to choose an outfit.

I inwardly groan again before quickly turning, exiting the room to wait for her in the living room.

Chapter Four

VERO

The drive over to his parent's house is tense. It's Saturday, it should be a relaxing day. I'm getting a little nervous feeding off Akmal's nervousness. *Eesh.* Is his family that bad? Am I missing something?

"You need to relax, Akmal. You're killing me. I'm getting your nervous vibes all over me."

We pull up to a large one-story home with a fairly large front yard. Once the car is in park, Akmal looks over at me from head to toe and takes a big gulp. What is up with him? I can't stand this nervous energy.

"Spit it out. What? Why are you looking at me like that? Is there something wrong with what I'm wearing?" I do a double take at my outfit while I'm sitting here. I think I look alright. My pencil skirt is down to my calf, my cardigan sweater is buttoned up all the way. Well, the top few look like they're about to cry, but they're holding on. I haven't dressed this covered in a while. I look like a damn librarian for crying out loud.

Akmal lets out a deep breath beside me and I can feel my face scowling at him. *What?*

"You look fucking beautiful, Vero. It's just..." I'm internally preening and cringing at the same time. Spit it out!

"The women of my culture dress a little more...more..."

"Just say it already! You're killing me here."

"I-I'm just a man, Vero. I don't claim to be an expert on women whatsoever. But please excuse anything that might make you uncomfortable from this point forward and do not hesitate to ask me anything, okay? We can do this." He lets out a long breath before repeating his last sentence. Maybe more for himself than me. "We can do this."

Akmal gets out the driver's side and runs around the car to open the passenger door for me. My heart pitter patters just a little bit at that, but I'm still not sure where I went wrong and he wasn't being very clear in the car about it. Feeling a little self-conscious now, I make sure to pull my skirt down as far as it will go before following his lead towards the house.

It's a beautiful and fairly large one-story home with a terracotta roof. I assume his sisters live here too. He had three from what I remember when they came by and helped clean Mat's apartment. The windows in the front look like they're covered by white lace curtains on the inside, but you can't see through it, much to my dismay.

So I can't tell if we're being watched while we're walking up the path towards the front door or not. Not sure if I should be grateful or more nervous about that fact.

We reached the door and the moment Akmal knocks once, it swings open pulling my hair in front of my face. I guess they were waiting for us after all.

"Akmal! You made it." Her eyes go to me. "The day I've prayed-"

"Ibu!" Akmal's reflexes catch his mother right before she hits the ground. I can hear the feminine screams coming from inside the home and a man, who I assume to be Akmal's father, comes rushing out.

Did she just faint? What happened? We haven't even made it through the door yet.

"Aye! Ling! Are you okay? What happened?" His father has taken his mother from his embrace and is rocking her. A groan escapes her lips as she comes to and I let out a breath. My heart almost stopped when I saw her go down. *My god.*

I put a hand on Akmal's arm in reassurance and it is like time stops. His mother, who just opened her eyes, turns her sight to where I am touching Akmal. Everyone's eyes are zoned in on where I'm touching Akmal. You can hear a damn pin drop.

Removing my hand like I just got burned, I fold them together in front of me to prevent myself from touching him any further. My cheeks are burning from their scrutiny and I can't tell if they're happy or mad about it.

"The day I've prayed for has finally been answered! Come, come." Like it never happened, this small woman who looks like she's wrapped from head to toe in fabric, gets up and hugs her son then turns to look at me.

Her smile is still bright as she pulls me in for a hug too. "Come, come! There is plenty of food. Everyone has been waiting for you."

She's pulling me inside before I can even say my own hellos. It's a good thing I wore flats today or I'd be falling flat on my face right now.

"Vero!" Akmal's harsh whisper makes me whip my face around. "Take off your shoes!"

It's then I notice the pile of shoes outside the front door and everyone inside barefoot. Quickly toeing them off without tripping, I let Akmal's mother drag me further inside.

"Ayah!! Akmal is here and he brought home a woman, huh! Tell your aunties! Hasanah! There is no Mat today. Aye, it's okay. I need you to start making the wedding list la."

I turn to look at Akmal, and all he does is shrug his shoulders with a sheepish smile. What am I missing here?

We reach what looks like the living room and there is a large spread of food and multiple dishes on the floor. In fact, after glancing around a few times, I don't see a dining room table in sight. Do they eat on the floor?

His mother is ushering me near the oldest daughter and comes to sit down between Akmal and me. It's a good thing my skirt has some stretch to it because I'm forced to sit with my legs to the side.

"Hi, I'm Hasanah."

"Vero." I smile at Akmal's sister. She looks to be the oldest of the three. Is this the one his mother wanted to set up with Mat? I need to tell Atsuko the next time I see her. I wonder if she knows.

There's an array of food and the house smells great. I'm reaching out to grab some of the food when Akmal's mom halts my hand. Looking up, I see everyone looking towards his father as he says a small prayer with his hands out like he's about to cup some water. *Oops.*

"Bismillah."

Suddenly everyone around me is murmuring the same word. Oh dear, I'm going to have to spank Akmal for not telling me all these important details. I'm getting kind of embarrassed.

I'm handed a bowl of food but now I'm scared to ask where the utensils are. I hear a masculine throat clearing and my eyes shoot to Akmal's automatically to see him signaling something to me with his eyes.

I watch as he eats with his hands. *His hands*! Shit, but this girl isn't a quitter. When in Rome and all that. Plus, Akmal's mother is staring at me with a large smile on her face like she's waiting for me to taste her food.

Monkey see, monkey do. I bring the food to my mouth and taste the different flavors. I accidentally bite my tongue and a "shit" comes out of my mouth. I hear feminine gasps from my right and see Akmal's mother with her hand over her heart to my right. I'm shooting apologetic looks at everyone but stare daggers at Akmal. He should have warned me! Too many years in the hood, cussing is almost part of my life blood. I'm going to have to make an effort to rein it in around his family who are probably starting to get scandalized by my uncouth behavior.

The pain from the bite dulls down and I continue to eat. It really is good and I'm still chewing when Akmal's mother leans into me and says, "It's good huh? Makan, makan." She says this right before she adds even more food onto my plate.

My eyes widen but I try my best to act natural. I mean, it's no different than my mother trying to stuff my face when I come over, right? Abuela is even worse than this. With that thought, I relax a little. Akmal's family is kind of endearing, actually.

Once our faces are stuffed and everyone starts slowing down, I figured I'd stop too. Bending over, I reach to put my dish down when it happens.

The two buttons on top that were crying pop off, and my ample cleavage starts peeking out through my cardigan. I hear gasps and someone is choking on their food when I hear Akmal clearing his throat a few times.

A hand touches my right arm and I turn to see Hasanah tilt her head to indicate I should follow her.

How fucking embarrassing. I mean, I'm never embarrassed of the girls, they're one of my pride and joys, but the current moment and mood is making me feel like I should go hide under a damn rock with my figure.

Hasanah takes my hand and leads me to a bedroom. It must be hers.

"Here, take this." It looks like a scarf. Wrapping it around my neck, I tuck the ends under the scoop of my cardigan and flatten the fabric out. Now I look like a fifties librarian who just came back from an episode of Outlander. Good grief. Standing in front of her full-length mirror, I make sure the girls are tucked safely away from innocent eyes.

Now that the problem has been fixed, Hasanah and I walk out of the bedroom only to hear her mother dramatically cry, "Haiyo, my son. She is not what I expected. Akmal, you need to buy her new clothes. Aye, that's okay. Once you are married there will be plenty of time. Make sure you take care of that."

Take care of 'that', 'not what she expected'? I'm not liking the sound of how she's describing my choice of attire as well as how she's talking about me. What's wrong with *me*? I mean, I'm not a skinny woman, and my curves usually come out to play. I've been more than good this whole time, haven't I? I usually never restrain myself back like this.

I need to make a good impression though. Hasanah and I look at each other. Hasanah has a sheepish look on her face that tells me this isn't the first time her mother has expressed opinions like this.

"Does your mother hate me?"

"Ah, it's not that. I mean, it's complicated. Sometimes, Malaysian elders like for their children to... You know?"

I'm in over my head because I damn well *don't know* what the hell is going on. "No, I don't. You're going to have to dumb it down for me."

Hasanah has a sheepish look on her face again. What's going on?

"Sometimes Malaysian parents like for their children to marry... nice girls like Malaysian girls." My eyes widen at that statement and my heart starts to beat a little harder. I don't know if I'm upset, mad or sad.

Hasanah puts her hands out and tries to put on a smile when she says, "No! I mean, it's not you. Really. It's just, culture sometimes runs deep, you know? But I'm sure my mother is already dying to set up the wedding, she probably doesn't care about that. She's waited a long time for this moment for Akmal."

We're halfway back to the living room when I hear Akmal's voice.

"Ibu, don't talk about her like that. I'm going to marry her, she's the only one I've ever wanted. Please respect her, even if she's not in the same room."

"Ah Akmal, Ibu didn't mean anything by it, you know. She is just worried about you and wants you to make good decisions. You could have found a good Malaysian girl any time. We didn't want you to be single this long." His dad wanted him to find a good Malaysian girl, huh?

"Bapa, I don't want a good Malaysian girl. I want the woman I'm going to marry, and she is here today. So please, hold back your comments. This is exactly why I couldn't live here anymore."

"Akmal, I didn't mean it like that. Malaysian or not, it is fine whoever you choose. But you must buy her some modest clothes la."

"Aye, tsk tsk tsk. Relax. We make the wedding arrangements and invite everyone. It will be fine. I already told your sisters to tell your aunts so they can spread the invitations. You need to marry her soon. We should have the wedding-"

Hasanah and I step into the living room and the conversation quiets. I don't know how I feel about all this. Does Akmal's mother hate me or not? Sounds like she's more excited about the wedding than who's getting married.

I'm not sure if we should overstay our welcome. I mean, that's how I'm feeling right now.

"Akmal, I think we should go, if that's okay?"

Chapter Five

AKMAL

My mother is acting like Vero is unsophisticated when it's far from the truth. "Ibu, don't talk about her like that. I'm going to marry her, she's the only one I've ever wanted. Please respect her, even if she's not in the same room." I feel possessive over her even if she probably won't agree to continue with the marriage after what's happened. Who could blame her? Her breasts are fucking beautiful and just can't be contained.

"Ah Akmal, Ibu didn't mean anything by it, you know. She is just worried about you and wants you to make good decisions. You could have found a good Malaysian girl any time. We didn't want you to be single this long." All these 'good Malaysian' girls are not Vero. She's the only one I've ever wanted so none of this matters.

"Bapa, I don't want a good Malaysian girl. I want the woman I'm going to marry, and she is here today. So please, hold back your comments. This is exactly why I couldn't live here anymore."

"Akmal, I didn't mean it like that. Malaysian or not, it is fine whoever you choose. But you must buy her some modest clothes." It's a crime to cover all that beauty up. But I understand that my parents are traditional and conservative when it comes to clothing. I'm going to have to find a middle ground on this. I need to show Vero I can take care of her, make her comfortable.

"Aye, tsk tsk tsk. Relax. We make the wedding arrangements and invite everyone. It will be fine. I already told your sisters to tell your aunts so they can spread the invitations. You need to marry her soon. We should have the wedding-"

The sound of someone entering the living room makes me turn. *Damn, she's beautiful.* From the top of her beautiful dark hair to her voluptuous body down to her little toes. She was carved by the heavens and she's all fucking mine. I need to make sure nothing happens from this point forward to make her want to break off this engagement.

Vero steps out with my sister and I can't take my eyes off the way she moves. My hands itch to touch her, to hold her and make sure she's real.

Her eyes lock on mine and they look unsure. My gut churns at how she's probably feeling right now. My family can be a bit overwhelming.

"Akmal, I think we should go, if that's okay?" Her wish is my command. I'm already ushering her towards the front door with my palm at the small of her back when it bursts open. Dammit, I'm too late.

"Aye! Akmal, you brought home a woman!"

"Akmal! Finally, the day has come! Let me measure her la!"

"Oh my. I need more fabric huh! Adila! Where is the measuring tape?"

"Ayo Akmal, she is so pretty. Irina, the tape is right here. I said I was going to measure her. Listen aye. Go, move her to the living room so we can get started."

I don't even know when I started holding Vero's hand but she's giving me a death grip. My aunties are coming through the door in a flurry with bolts of fabric in their arms and who knows what else. How did they get here that fast?

"Aye, you finally made it. Come, come. Let's get her to the living room. Hidaya! Sakinah! Start on the list and invitations. Don't forget my friends and Ayah's friends! I need to see the list before it's done."

I run my hand down my face because I knew it would be this way. Shit. Looking over to Vero, she looks like a deer caught in headlights. I've never seen her so quiet.

Squeezing her hand, she looks up at me and I just want to kiss the look away. I'm surprised she hasn't broken off the engagement yet.

"It will be okay. They've been waiting for the day to put a wedding together. That's my Auntie Irina and Adila." I indicate Auntie Irina in the red and Auntie Adila in the purple. I highly doubt Vero is going to remember everyone's names by the time it's all said and done.

"Tsk tsk tsk." My mother is doing her signature head shake. "Akmal, what kind of son are you? You never even told me my daughter-in-law's name. How am I supposed to speak with her huh?"

She slaps me upside the head and I send a sheepish glance to Vero. Ibu is right, I never did introduce her correctly.

"Sorry Ibu. Ibu, Bapa, Auntie Irina, Auntie Adila, this is Vero..."

"Veronica Hernandez, but you can call me Vero." I never knew her real name, I've always just called her Vero. The thought sobers me and reminds me of the situation I'm in. Trying to convince the woman of my dreams to go through with a Malaysian wedding.

"Akmal! Have you been hiding her from us huh? My goodness, why do you worry us like that?"

"Akmal! Walao eh. My god. You're finally getting married. I thought you were going to die alone."

"What are you talking about dying alone huh? You took longer than Akmal before Adila agreed to marry your sorry self."

I internally groan because it's never going to end. The whole family is coming. Hidaya and Sakinah are probably calling everyone in the vicinity as we speak at my mother's behest.

"This is my Uncle Tuah and Uncle Zaka. Married to Irina and Adila."

"I don't think I'm going to remember everyone's name."

My poor Vero. "It's okay, you'll remember them later." I almost don't even get to finish my sentence before my aunties pull her away from me and start restraining her with a measuring tape.

"Akmal!" Vero is whisper-yelling at me and I'm about to whisk her away when my uncles pull me farther from her in the opposite direction.

"Akmal, we need to celebrate this day! I didn't think it would come. I was placing a bet with Zaka to see if you would end up a bachelor. Zaka, now you have to clean my garage!"

"Let the women do what they need to do, they're going to pull you next for measurements. Come, come. Tell us how you met this cantik woman. Tuah! Look at her. Who knew a woman like her would go for our Akmal, huh?"

"Akmal! You did good. Marry her quickly before she realizes what she's gotten herself into."

Internally groaning, I rub my hand down my face as my uncles continue to talk about how unworthy I am of a woman like Vero.

I already know I am.

VERO

Akmal's aunts are putting me through the wringer. I don't know what's happening but suddenly they have my measurements, placing fabrics against my skin and have already picked out the wedding decor with Akmal's mother.

My eyes are searching him out for a rescue but his uncles must have taken him to another room. I miss him. I miss his calm. I'm getting kind of antsy and I don't like it but I'm putting on a smile for the sake of his family. Damn, even Vegas is easier than this. We should just elope and call it a day.

The aunties are shaking their heads when they measure my breasts and hips making me feel self-conscious again.

"Hidaya! Call Akmal in here so we can measure him!"

"Sakinah, did you get the family list yet? Let me see."

"Hasanah! Did Mat ask you to marry him yet? If you wait too long you are going to die alone huh."

Oh, I need to nip this one in the butt because I can just see Atsuko throwing punches where she doesn't need to be.

"Mat is already engaged."

The entire living room goes silent and I think I hear Hasanah clearing her throat.

"What?! Mat is already engaged? How? Hasanah! I told you that you needed to grab him while he was still single, aye!"

"Ibu! I always knew Mat wasn't into me. It was you who kept pushing him. Leave him alone. Let him be happy."

"Hasanah! I want *you* to be happy, that is why I need you to get married. Haiyah!" Her mother is muttering something Malaysian under her breath that I can't understand. Or do they call it Malay? But it sounds like she's going off on Hasanah judging by the frustrated look on her face.

I have to be in the twilight zone right now. Akmal and I cross paths for a second before his aunts are measuring him in the same fabrics in a flurry of movements.

I can still hear Akmal's mother and sister bickering, but the moment his aunts let him out of their grasp is the moment I grab onto his hand. I need some air. I can only take so much. Begging him with my eyes, Akmal's expression softens before he announces our exit.

When we get back into the car and shut the door, I let out an exasperated breath. *Holy hell, what just happened in there?*

We end up driving home in complete silence. We're both probably exhausted from the day's events and it was just lunch with the family. Am I going to be able to handle this? They say you don't just marry the person, you marry the family as well.

Akmal puts the car in park when we reach the apartment. Turning my head to look at him, my heart skips a beat and my brain tells me that yes, I'm going through with this because Akmal is worth it.

I guess I need to tell my parents about my impromptu engagement, huh? Akmal opens the passenger door for me with a soft smile and grabs my hand before leading us to our apartment. Wow, this is new. I kind of like it. His hand in mine makes me feel things. Good things.

We walk into the front door and he lets go of my hand. I already feel the loss of his warmth but I take a deep breath in and out to suck in the warmth of our home. *Our* home. My old apartment with Atsuko still has a week to go before the lease is up, but I can't find it in myself to care. Not when Akmal has that look in his eyes where it seems like he is fighting an internal battle about what to do with me.

"I need to tell my parents about our engagement." His expression doesn't change.

"Yes, you should."

The tension builds between us as the silence grows louder with each moment that passes by. I don't know what I'm allowed to do now that we're engaged. My pussy is telling me to go to town, but my mind is telling me that I need to see Akmal's culture through. To make sure I make it right in the eyes of his family. I need to be a good girl right now. A good girl that waits for her prize.

I'm not even controlling my legs when they walk towards him. His eyes shine with desire as we're standing face to face with only millimeters to separate us. Running my hands along his arms, I take a deep breath and close my eyes to just soak in the peace our home brings us. The masculine smell of my man.

I'm only about five-feet-five in height to Akmal's five-feet-seven but I love it. Grabbing the front of his shirt, I bring his face down to mine but stop when our lips are only a breath apart. Rubbing my nose against his, I soak in his warmth. My inner ho is crying, crying for something more between us but I need to resist.

This has to be the hardest thing I've ever done.

I let him go and turn to walk away.

Chapter Six

VERO

I haven't visited my parents in a couple of weeks but I feel good about this, about us. Akmal is all nerves as we pull into my childhood neighborhood. Yards get smaller and bars on the windows start becoming rampant as we drive deeper into the neighborhood. To the untrained eye, it looks like you need to start locking your car doors. To the eyes of those who grew up in these streets, this is home.

Pulling up into the driveway behind the 1970 Chevelle SS, I put the car in park as we step out. My mother is already opening up the screen door with her other hand on her hip. My heart warms as I watch my mother stand there with a smile on her face.

"¿Mira, mira quien viene? Milagro que se acuerda que tiene familia." She always gives me sass if I don't come by every damn day. I'm here now, aren't I?

"Mamá. Don't be like that. You know I would never forget my family. La bendición." She's right. I haven't asked for blessing in a while. I probably should visit more often.

"Que Dios te bendiga. Hija! You finally decide to stop by and didn't even tell me you were bringing a boy home. It's okay, I made enough for everyone. Come in, come in."

"Mamá, you always have plenty of comida, that's why I didn't tell you I was bringing someone over."

She eyes me skeptically and then stares at Akmal. "¿Quién es tu amigo?"

"Esto es Akmal."

"¿Porque you no call me por una semana? How would I know if you're alive? Tu papá estaba preocupado. He thought you died."

We're already walking through the doorway when Akmal bows towards my mother. I give her a kiss on the cheek as I continue to tell her, "You know you don't have to worry about me. I've been living on my own just fine. I'm not starving, mira mi culo." Bumping her hips with said ass, I try to hold back a laugh.

My mother swats my ass as I walk inside to be greeted by my dad who has an unsure look on his face as he sizes up Akmal, especially after his little bow.

"La bendición papá."

"Dios te bendiga...¿Mira, mira quien viene? Vero, ¿Quién es tu amigo?" I swear my mom and dad are really just one person.

"Vero! It's about fucking time you came home to check on Mamá y Papá. Are you too good for us now, or what?"

My older brother, Fabian, wraps his arms around my neck in a headlock like we're seven again. I swear this fucker never grows up. He's gotten a little bigger since the last time I saw him. He must be working out or something. Despite standing almost a head and a half taller than me, I elbow him in the abs hard. He pretends to be hurt and lets go like he's so damn offended at my audacity. At least he didn't mess up my hair.

"Puta, you almost messed up my hair."

My dad slaps Fabian upside the head while my mom slaps me on the ass.

"Mira tu boca! We have company." My dad is still eyeing Akmal warily, who's been standing there quietly watching how my crazy family interacts. I probably should be embarrassed, but this is mi familia. We never hide who we are.

Taking a big whiff of air, it smells like my mom made some empanadillas. I'm suddenly fucking starving. My nose is already leading my legs where they need to go when I hear Fabian's loud-ass voice speaking to me.

"Vero, ¿Quién es tu novio?" Oh shit, that's right. I got a little caught up with being home again and smelling deliciousness that I forgot to introduce my man.

"Familia, esto es Akmal. He's my fiancé. We're getting married!" I grab Akmal's arm and pull him towards me for a semi hug. He looks really nervous if his hand scratching the back of his head is anything to go by. He's so cute.

My face is hurting from how hard I'm smiling up at my man.

"Vero, ven a hablar conmigo por favor. It is very nice to meet you Akmal. Siéntate por favor." My mom is already pulling me away for 'a talk' but not before I point my finger at Fabian.

"Fabian, be good." I'm staring daggers at him as I watch my dad and brother surround poor Akmal. I forgot to tell him I'm the only girl in the family.

We reach the far side of the kitchen when my mom turns to me.

"When did you meet this boy? I've never seen you bring anyone home and now you tell me tienes esposo. How long have you been hiding him? How come you didn't tell tu familia? You just go off and get married? I don't even know what kind of family he comes from."

"Mamá, please understand. We're not married *yet*. Quit being dramatic." I slap her arm for emphasis since she has both hands on her hips like she's scolding me. I'm not eighteen anymore, I'm thirty-three.

"Akmal is different. He's Malaysian and his culture says he can't date. He needs to get married before he can do anything. Es un buen chico, Mamá. Believe me when I say that, you know me."

My mom stares at me like she's about to cry. I'm still trying to decide if these are happy tears or sad tears.

"What do you mean? Explícamelo." How do I explain to my mother Akmal's strict upbringing and cultural rules? It's so far from what we know.

"Mamá, you wouldn't believe me even if I told you. Pero, trust me on this. I've never been more sure in my life. He's the one Mamá. He's different." My mom watches my face closely.

"How come you couldn't want un buen chico puertorriqueño?" She's always getting on me about finding a good Puerto Rican boy.

"Mamá!" I hit her again before a small smile graces her face. She knows the commitment issues I've had since my high school sweetheart. She was the one who was there for me when my world came crashing down. That boy was hispanic and honestly, I'm not that inclined to visit that again. Akmal is a damn dream come true.

"I've never seen you like this before."

"Like what?"

"Hija, you glow when you talk about him." I feel like I'm glowing every time I'm around him. I didn't know it was that obvious.

"Mamá, he's different. I-I didn't think the day would come for me. I didn't think a man like him would be in my life." I sigh and feel myself smiling once more just thinking about him. "He's one in a million."

"¿Estás embarazada?"

"What? No, I'm not pregnant! I just told you Akmal's culture doesn't even let us touch when we date." She narrows her eyes at me like she's got x-ray vision and can see the truth through my stomach.

"Mamá!"

"I just want you to be happy, Hija." She stares at me again but her hard expression finally begins to crack. Her hands caress my face in a really tender gesture that makes my heart feel like it's going to overflow. I love my mom. I'm sticking to my guns, Akmal is the man for me. Just thinking about him makes my cheeks widen again.

"If he can make you happy like this already, I'm happy for you." Dammit, I didn't wear any waterproof mascara and I can feel my damn eyes watering. Was I really miserable that long for her to see the difference so clearly?

She pulls me into a firm hug and I breathe in my mom's scent deeply, trying to stave away the tears before it makes me look like a hot mess.

"Vamos, antes tu papá y hermano says something stupid and chases your man away. Pero if he was un buen chico puertorriqueño, he wouldn't be scared off."

"Mamá!"

She's right. My dad can be overprotective sometimes because I'm his little girl. Fabian can be overprotective sometimes because of what happened with my last serious boyfriend. I never did find out if Fabian did anything to Roman after he found out what he did to me. But Fabian came home late that night and was drinking and smashing things before he left again. Despite being older than me by three years, at thirty-six, Fabian and I are still close.

"What the hell are you guys doing to my man?"

Both my dad and Fabian are standing in front of Akmal who is sitting in the chair looking like he's being interrogated for country secrets. My dad's got his arms crossed looking like a damn cholo about to bust a cap.

"We're just getting to know each other, aren't we Akmal. That's your real name, right?" I elbow Fabian in the ribs again before sitting my ass right onto Akmal's lap to ward away the guard dogs.

"Why did you keep this from me, Hija? It breaks my heart. You know I love you and you're my favorite daughter."

"Pfft. I'm your only daughter Papá. I'm not hiding anything. It all happened really fast. But he's the one, so be nice." My dad literally looks like his world is shattering. I'm his baby girl and he's probably afraid I'll never come back home to visit again. Everyone in this house is so damn dramatico.

"Papá, don't be dramatic. You know you're my number one man. I'll always come back to visit, I won't forget you."

"Vero, how about me huh? You going to leave me behind? You're my favorite sister."

"Puta, I'm your only sister."

"Exactly!"

"What is that supposed to mean, exactly?"

"Aye, silencio. Everybody sit down so we can eat. The food is getting cold while you guys are acting like babies."

"You can't be seria, Maria. This is the first time Vero is even bringing the guy around and suddenly mi hija is getting married?" Dammit, now my dad is staring at my stomach too. "¿Estás embarazada?"

"No! I'm not pregnant! Stop asking me!"

"What the hell Vero, you didn't tell me you were pregnant!"

"Shut up, Fabian. I just said I wasn't pregnant. Open your damn ears!"

My mom shoots a glare at my dad as she raises a wooden spatula to his face. *Uh-oh.*

"Don't forget how you stole me away from mi familia. You came into mi casa and told my dad you were going to marry me. I was sixteen, Alejandro. He thought I was pregnant too." My dad shut up then. I've never seen his face so red. You go, Mamá. Damn, I almost forgot this story. Sixteen, *eesh.*

"Maria, don't be like that. You were the only one for me."

"Alejandro, Vero says Akmal is the only one for her. Deal with it! Even though he's not un buen chico puertorriqueño." Ugh! Can she just not let that go!? I know he's not a damn Puerto Rican boy.

"Akmal, what are you? Are you Asian or something?" I slap Fabian up the back of his head. How rude! "Vero, I'm just asking. Damn. How am I supposed to know if I don't ask? Dramatica."

"Akmal is Malaysian." Both my dad and brother have the most confused look on their faces. It makes me want to laugh. "Yes, you can say he's Asian."

My dad and brother start nodding their heads.

"So he's the one huh. Vero, you sure? I know my buddy at work is still trying to get you to notice him. He's a nice guy, I trust him. You want his number?"

"Fucker, listen!" I point my finger right at his face even though he's sitting across from me and shoot him a look. "Akmal is the only one! I don't want any of your buddies hitting me up. I know the crowd you hang out with, Fabian!"

"What is that supposed to mean? I'm a good guy, I only surround myself with good guys." This fool right here. Fabian has been in and out of trouble ever since I can remember. Looking back, I'm honestly surprised Roman is still alive. My brother is known in the hood for his temper and reputation.

But at home, he's just Fabian. Overprotective big brother with a big-ass mouth that doesn't know when to shut up. That's why I fucking love him.

My mom shuts everyone up when she places the food on the table. I grab Akmal's hand and squeeze it for reassurance. He probably thinks we're a bunch of heathens.

"Are you alright?" Akmal gives me a small smile in response to my question and my heart settles a little. Good, the Hernandez family didn't send him running for the hills.

"Yeah, I'm just not used to...your family. But I'm good." Sending an air kiss his way, I let go of his hand as we prepare to eat the delicious meal my mom made for us all. Damn, look at this spread. My stomach is growling with all these smells.

My mom slaps my hand as she walks towards her chair. I'm starving. How can she put this all in front of me and expect me to wait?

Once my mom is seated and comfortable, my dad says 'Buen provecho' and we're digging in. Akmal looks a little lost, so I take it upon myself to fill his plate with some arroz con pollo and whatever else I think he would like. Chicken and rice isn't too far off from what I had at his parents' house. He sends me an appreciative glance before we start eating. The thing about my family is that we take our sweet time to eat and enjoy the tastes we're putting into our mouths.

I miss this sometimes, sitting together like this. But that was when I was single, now I'm not. I can't wait to see what kind of traditions Akmal and I will make together. I can start inviting mi familia over to our place. The thought sends warm tingles to my belly. I really am excited about this marriage. That and I don't know how long I can restrain myself from jumping his damn bones.

Now that I'm thinking of him, my hand runs across his thigh under the table and Akmal chokes on his food.

Rubbing his back, I pretend I'm surprised. "Baby, are you okay?"

"Is there something wrong con mi comida?"

"Mamá, you know your food is the best. Stop thinking like that. It probably just went down the wrong pipe." I'm still rubbing his back when Akmal sends me a sheepish look. Poor thing. I better get him out of here soon before it gets too weird for him.

Lunch was a nice affair. Everyone starts asking Akmal about his culture and religion. When it comes to the wedding, he can't answer much since his mother has taken over all the duties.

"At least we're getting invited to the wedding. Pinche Vero."

"Of course mi familia is going to the wedding. What kind of person do you think I am?"

"I don't know, Vero, I leave work to visit mi familia and all of a sudden my sister is basically already married."

"I'm not married *yet*, Fabian."

"Almost!"

"You two quit fighting. Let's finish this meal in some peace huh?"

"Si, Mamá."

"Si, Mamá."

"So Akmal, when can we meet your family?"

I can see Akmal's hands shaking on his thigh. Placing mine over his, I give him an encouraging smile.

He clears his throat a few times before he answers my dad. "Whenever you'd like, sir. I mean, my mother is probably setting up the wedding for the coming weekend as we speak."

"We come over on Tuesday then." My mom nods her head like she has the right to have the final say. I tell ya. That at least gives us one day to be alone together before the clash of the titans.

Chapter Seven

AKMAL

I don't know how this meeting of the families will go and it makes me nervous. Vero's been telling me to relax but I just can't. It's still early and I'm sitting at the breakfast table with my mind running through the many possible disasters that might happen tomorrow.

It also doesn't help that Vero is walking about in a damn tank top and thong. She's going to kill me, I just know it.

She bends over to get something out of the fridge and I groan, rubbing my hand down my face, wishing I could be rubbing something else. If not her, at least my dick that's crying behind my shorts. But I can't.

"Vero..."

When I open my eyes, she's a breath away from my face with a seductive smile that pulls me in like a fish on a hook. She's so fucking beautiful in her confidence. But this angle doesn't help my situation one bit because she's bent over just enough to make it look like her breasts are about to fall out of her thin tank top. I should be used to this by now, right? She's like this around me every damn day since she's been here. Is she doing this to me on purpose?

"Yes, Akmal."

"...You're killing me."

"How so?" Her finger starts trailing down her cleavage and I almost cum right there. Dammit, she *is* doing this on purpose. I love it and I hate it.

The next thing I know, she sits on my lap facing me and I feel like I'm stuck between a rock and a hard place. Or in this case, my rock hard cock stuck between our clothing, crying for where it really wants to go.

Vero grinds forward and I hiss. Shit, how can it still feel so good when we're both fully dressed? Well, I'm fully dressed.

"Vero." Her name comes out almost in a growl as I try to tamp down my desires before I embarrass myself. I can't find it in me to push her off. Just the thought of her sliding against my cock again makes it twitch.

Vero gives a little intake of air before she leans forward. I lean my head back as far as I can go in a half-assed attempt to get away and close my eyes. Shit, we shouldn't be doing this.

Her warm breath fans across the side of my face as she whispers into my ear. "Are you happy to see me, Akmal?"

Through gritted teeth, I try to answer her as civil as I can so as to not push her any further. "I'm always happy to see you."

Her low chuckle does something to me. The way her soft breasts push against my chest makes my cock weep in frustration. The warmth of her body on mine makes me think very nasty thoughts. Thoughts a good Malay boy should not be thinking. Opening my eyes, I stare at the ceiling to try and gain some semblance of control.

Think unsexy thoughts. Think unsexy thoughts.

My mother's voice floats through my mind, reminding me I need to buy Vero more appropriate clothing. The thought disappears when I feel her shift on top of me.

I can feel her hard nipples rubbing against my chest when I finally gain the strength to put some space between us with my hands pushing her away. Fuck, her skin is so soft and she smells like a wet dream come true, feminine and enticing.

"Vero, we need to go shopping before we meet my parents again."

"What's wrong with the clothes I have?"

"Nothing's wrong with them. You look absolutely beautiful in them, but my culture tends to lean more towards the ... conservative side."

She crosses her arms and it only serves to push her breasts even closer towards me, making me swallow the large lump in my throat. *My god, what would it feel like to rub my face against all that? What would it feel like to taste that...*

"Look, I'm sorry about what happened last time. It wasn't my fault. At least it didn't happen when your uncles were there."

A growl comes out of my throat before I realize it. Just thinking about my uncles looking at her that way makes me irrationally angry.

"No one is allowed to see what's mine."

Vero goes quiet as her eyes widen a fraction. I'm trying to calm my damn nerves when her arms slowly go around my shoulders. How am I supposed to stay away from this for a whole damn week? This wedding needs to hurry the fuck up.

Vero leans in to rub her breasts on me again and it makes me shudder. My strength is shattering by the minute and I am too damn selfish to push her off again. My hands have a mind of their own as they slowly grip her hips, making her grind down on me again in response.

Leaning my head back once more, I groan in this never ending frustration which was my mistake because Vero takes that exact moment of weakness and starts to lick and kiss my neck. Damn this woman!

"Vero... we can't."

"I know, but sometimes I just need to touch you. To make sure you're real and that you're mine. I can't help the way you make me feel, Akmal. It's been hard for me too. Almost as hard as your cock between my legs right now." My fucking god, the mouth on this woman. She makes me want to do nasty things to her, things I've only seen in my fantasies.

I don't know if she's grinding down on me or if I'm grinding up against her, but suddenly there's a steady, slow rhythm forming between us on this kitchen chair.

The temperature in the room is getting hotter, the air is getting thicker and my nerves are fraying, hanging by a thread.

No sane hot-blooded man would be able to deny this goddess right here, not like this. Fuck, there shouldn't be *any* man but me with this goddess right here. Just the thought of another guy touching what's mine makes me grip her hips harder as I continue to grind into her hot center. I can feel her wetness soaking through my thin shorts and my mind starts to slowly enter a lustful haze, making me drunk off this moment between us.

I don't know who went towards who, but our lips start lightly grazing against each other. We're both fighting and giving in at the same time, unsure when to let our primal instincts go. It makes me delirious knowing I can do that to her too, sending her into a lustful haze just like the one I'm currently drowning in. When my hand starts to trail up her sides on its own accord, something snaps and our lips crash together in a forbidden dance.

I've never kissed anyone but Vero before. I should be embarrassed at my lack of experience but the way she moans into my mouth tells me she likes what I'm giving, making me gain more confidence by the second. Making me more selfish with what she's willing to give me.

She must be a goddess with the way she invokes these things from me, creating me into a person I don't recognize. When her breath hitches, I feel powerful; I feel in control even though I know I'm not. I'm the one who's under her spell.

We're grinding so hard together that we're probably wearing the fabric of my shorts thinner. I should stop. We shouldn't do this. But she makes me too weak...and too strong at the same time. I want to be her weakness too. Make her want me the way I want her.

Her fingers thread through my hair as our tongues fight for something we shouldn't have right now. Does it make it even more enticing that we both know we're doing something we shouldn't?

Vero suddenly shudders and cries into my mouth as she grinds down in an erratic rhythm. I feel like I'm on top of the fucking world, a man that's completed his mission with the orgasm I gave her. Me, virgin Akmal, made this woman cry out in ecstasy. She kisses me like she knows this moment between us won't last. The thought alone makes us both frantic in our tangle of limbs.

The moment doesn't last because soon enough, lightning shoots down my spine as my balls tighten and I climax behind my shorts; the wetness pulls me out of this trance we've put ourselves in. The lust fog clears and the guilt starts to press down on me.

"Fuck. Vero, we can't do this anymore. We have to wait."

"Do you regret it?" She sounds so damn hurt it makes my chest ache.

"What? No!" Grabbing her face between my hands, I kiss her again because dammit, I can't help it. Breaking our liplock for much needed air, I press my forehead against hers. *Damn it all.* I just can't stop touching her, not now that I've had a taste.

"I want you so bad, I'm dying a little bit each day I have to wait." I let out a hard breath and close my eyes. It hurts to look at what I can't fucking have, not right now. My chest constricts at what I'm probably doing to her. Does she feel rejected? I don't know what else to do.

"..I know." She slowly removes herself and walks towards the bathroom door, closing it shut without another word.

"Fucking hell. What do I do?" I must be going insane because I'm talking to myself out loud, expecting some higher being to answer. *What do I fucking do?*

Dammit, I can't leave things like this. I'm supposed to be her man. I'm supposed to always make her feel loved like she's the queen of my entire world. Growling, I get up from the chair and walk my way towards the damn bathroom.

The sound of the water and the heat of the steam makes my insides feel something ugly. I don't like feeling like I did her wrong when we were just feeling so damn right together. Stripping out of my clothes quickly, I slide the shower door open and step inside with my back to the sprayer.

"Akmal!"

I love my name on her damn lips. I want to bury it inside of me the only way I can, the only way I know how for the time being. Pushing her up against the back of the shower, my lips come crashing down hard on hers. The feel of her wet body sliding against mine is a new experience, one I'll have to make sure to visit often once we're married and these shackles are taken off us.

We can't go all the way. We need to stay in control between these slips. My hand is itching to do so much more and the only way I know how to stop it is to grab hers and bring them up over her head where I know they can't cause anymore trouble.

Our kisses become frantic, like we're both starving instead of having just been together not ten minutes ago. The rushing of blood down to my groin makes me lightheaded, and when my dick comes up to graze against her pussy, I push myself away from her with a growl. Fuck! We need to stop.

Giving her one last chaste kiss on the lips, I try to regain my senses before speaking to her, my voice gravelly from the pain of holding back. "You've buried yourself in me so deeply, don't ever think I don't want you, Vero. This wedding can't come soon enough."

Turning around and quickly scrubbing myself of the evidence of what just happened at the breakfast table, I slide the shower door probably harder than necessary and make my exit, leaving dripping wet before I do anything else I shouldn't.

Grabbing a towel from the linen closet on the way to my room, I dry myself off quickly and get dressed in jerky movements. I'm feeling pissed. Pissed at myself for letting it go so far because now I'm addicted. I need to be strong.

Fully dressed, I sit on the couch in the living room to wait for Vero. I need to stick to the plan, I need to take her shopping to get her clothes. I need to stop thinking about her wet breasts and the way the water slides down her body. Shit, the more I think about it, the more I realize there was something glistening in her belly button. Leaning forward, I put my head in my hands and growl at my situation. I'm dying to find out if I saw what I saw. But if my face is that close to her, I won't be able to stop myself from smelling her and tasting her. Dammit, now my mouth is watering at the thought of her pussy against my lips and tongue.

"Akmal, I'm ready." Lifting my head, I see Vero in a beautiful dress that hugs her breasts and flares out to her knee. Just thinking about other men looking at how beautiful she is makes me angry again. Fuck, how am I supposed to contain something that just can't be contained? Why am I feeling so damn angry and out of control?

Standing up, I'm not sure what I should do. Do I make her order clothes online? What if she feels like I'm rejecting her company in public? What if other guys try to take what's mine? I can't hide her away forever, can I? I'm starting to go through all the ways I can do just that when Vero clears her throat, taking me out of my thoughts of ways to keep your potential wife captive until the wedding day.

"Akmal, are we going shopping or what? Why are you just standing there frowning?" The frown she throws at me makes me want to kiss her again. But if we do, we might not make it out. Shit, if we stay here even longer, I don't think I can make myself remain celibate. I mean, I'm still a virgin, right? Since I didn't actually stick my dick inside her hot pussy. Fuck, now I'm thinking about how hot her pussy was when my dick tried to say hello in the shower.

"Akmal!"

"Shit, sorry. You're too fucking beautiful and the thought of other guys seeing you shopping in that is making me crazy."

"In what? This? It's just a dress. It's not even hugging my curves."

Growling under my breath as I grab her hand to lead her out the door, I mumble to myself, "Men don't need tight clothes to imagine what's underneath."

Chapter Eight

VERO

We're back at our residence and Akmal came home so pissed, he had to go out with Mat to 'let out some steam' as he calls it. I remember Atsuko telling me that Mat goes to an MMA gym to keep a handle on his temper. I didn't think Akmal even had a temper. He's always been such a calm guy. Is it me? The thought makes me feel ugly inside.

Whatever, that means Atsuko is all mine for the time being.

Ding dong.

Speak of the she-devil, there she is! I feel like it's been ages since we've hung out. All this family stuff and tension is getting on my damn nerves. And before that was the whole Alfonso issue. Guess I can see why Akmal's been tense lately.

Opening the door, I can smell my BFF before I even see her.

"Vero!"

"Atsuko!"

We're screaming each other's names and hugging like we're separated twins. Damn, I miss her. Pulling her inside and kicking the door shut, I make sure to lock it before I drag her onto our couch to catch up.

"What have you been up to, chica!?" I'm running to the kitchen to grab us some water before planting my own ass down right next to her.

"Still doing my day job at the makeup counter. Mat keeps me pretty busy at home." Atsuko's face tells me exactly how Mat 'keeps her busy'. I'm so jealous.

"Aye, don't tell me that! I still can't do anything with Akmal even though we're basically engaged now."

"Wait, what?"

"Oh, that's right. It happened so fast, I never got a chance to tell you!"

"Bitch, tell me everything! What the hell?"

"Remember that plan I had?"

"Yeah? I'm guessing it worked, then? But what do you mean you still can't do anything with Akmal? You guys did something that night, right? How the hell did you get engaged so fast?"

Ugh, this thing between Akmal and I is so complicated. But I try my best to tell Atsuko everything from the proposal to meeting the families.

"And now mi familia wants to meet his familia tomorrow. I'm nervous but I'm not. You know how my family can be. What if Fabian can't filter the crap that comes out of his mouth and offends Akmal's family?"

"Yeah, I'd worry about Fabian."

"I'll just have to tear him a new one before we get there so he knows how fucking serious I am." My brother better not do anything to mess this up between the families. "This sexual tension between us is killing me though. I don't know what to do. My pussy says plow forward and take no survivors, but my mind is telling me I need to show Akmal how serious I am by trying to follow his culture. We're scrambling to put out the flames that keep growing between us."

"What happened today? I don't remember ever hearing about Akmal joining Mat at the gym. Is he alright?"

"Ugh, I don't know. I mean, he took me out shopping because apparently I don't dress modest enough for his family. I mean I get it, but how rude, right? So we're shopping and every time I bend over to look at something, Akmal is standing right behind me, almost rubbing his crotch on me. As if my vagina isn't hungry already!"

"Are you serious?" Atsuko is laughing at my misery right now, but I can't help but laugh too now that I'm thinking about it.

"Yes! When this male worker came to ask if I needed any help, you should have seen how Akmal cut him off with a 'we're fine, thank you' and glared at the back of the poor guy's head."

"How cute."

"I guess? But I mean, in the moment I was mad because I really don't know what I'm supposed to be buying and I really did need the help!"

Atsuko is full-on laughing now. "What did you guys do then? Did you get anything at all?"

"Girl, that man kept growling every time I tried to reach for something or get a closer look at something, that I started growling back! Like, what the hell? I need to make sure the fabric works well with my curves, you know? I can't restrict the girls, it's painful."

"They are some nice girls too."

"I know, right? I mean, it wasn't my fault they fell out during his family lunch."

Atsuko was just taking a drink when she starts choking. So dramatic.

"How the hell did your boobs fall out of your shirt? I know every article of clothing you have. What happened?"

"Ugh! I mean, I was trying to be modest. Remember that long sleeve cardigan I have? The one I usually wear open?"

"Oh, no. You didn't button it to the top, did you? Please tell me you didn't. How can you even button it? Why didn't you wear anything underneath?"

"I didn't think I needed to since I was covered like a damn virgin librarian! *Ugh!* For some reason, my hand reached for my light push up bra too, which as you know...pushes them up towards the buttons I had no business buttoning!"

Atsuko is full out laughing and rolling on the couch. This bitch!

"Stop laughing! I'm trying to tell you a damn story! So, we eat on the floor and I bend over to put the plate down when my buttons fly and the girls sigh."

We're both laughing like hyenas now until we finally get it out of our system. Damn, I miss being like this with Atsuko.

"What happened?"

"Akmal's family was scandalized, of course. At least Hasanah helped by giving me a scarf to kind of cover up. OH! I forgot to tell you, did you know Akmal's mother was trying to set up Hasanah with Mat?"

"What? No, Mat's never mentioned it." Atsuko is frowning and I don't want to lead her astray in her thoughts.

"I mean, from their argument during my fitting and measurements, it seemed that Hasanah wasn't interested in Mat. So don't go crazy on her or anything. She seemed like a nice girl who just so happens to have a mother who wants all her children to be married off quickly."

I'm not sure if it reduces her worries but her frown starts to lighten. Atsuko has become quite possessive of Mat ever since they almost got torn apart by bitches that had no business being in theirs. Now that I think about it, I wonder if there are bitches after my man too. The thought makes me want to scratch some eyes out and shove them down their hypothetical throats. I've worked too damn hard through all this tension to lose my man to some random ho.

"I'm going to tell Fabian to keep an eye out for hoes after my man tomorrow, in case I don't catch everything."

"How the hell is Fabian going to keep an eye out for the hoes? Lifting their skirts?"

We both laugh at that because it sounds like something he would volunteer for.

"No, that wouldn't be good. Malaysians are different, you know? I don't want to cause a huge scandal before I'm even allowed in the family."

"Do you even know the details about the wedding? Every time I even think of wedding details, I get a headache. There's so much that goes into it."

"Shit!" I bounce a little on the couch when an idea comes to my head. Atsuko startles at my little jump and slaps my shoulder.

"What the hell? Don't scare me like that. Why are you yelling?"

"I have an idea! Why don't you and Mat join us tomorrow? I mean, everyone seems to know Mat already. That way I don't need to ask Fabian to look for hoes. You can be my right-hand girl. Plus, you'll get to meet Hasanah and see that she's not after your man. Settle your worries because I know you got them since I've mentioned her. Don't lie!"

Atsuko makes a face, one I know means she agrees but doesn't want to agree. Too bad. She knows I'm right. It will be a win-win for all of us. "Yeah, I guess. When are you going back to work?"

I had called off work for a couple of weeks after the Alfonso incident. Had to make sure he was put away after his attempted rape with Atsuko. I also wanted to be in the right headspace before I go back to bartending. I'm glad I requested the time off too because look where we are now, planning a damn rush wedding.

"I think I have about a week and a half left."

"So you're going through with all this, huh? Damn, Vero. You and your YOLO lifestyle."

"Life is way too damn short, and I ain't letting no ho scoop up Akmal. That boy is mine. After all this sexual tension, I'm not coming up for air after we're married." And that's the damn truth.

"Are you using toys at all?"

"Fuck, I already broke my vibrators before he even asked me to marry him. After seeing his cock, I don't want a damn dildo, I want him."

The door opens halfway through my last sentence, and we both turn our heads to see the boys coming inside.

Akmal doesn't look any happier.

"Uh...we're back." Mat looks a little nervous. I'm trying to think back on what sentence they walked in on to make him look uncomfortable.

"Yeah...um, did you girls have a good time?" Akmal's got his pleasant face on, the one where he's trying to be peaceful and friendly around everyone. I've been around him long enough to finally know the difference now. The thought both warms me and makes me apprehensive because he's hiding his feelings.

"Mat, baby, how do you feel about going over to Akmal's family gathering tomorrow with Vero's family? Akmal, would that be okay?"

I'm still staring at Akmal's face, trying to figure out what's going on in his head when his expression goes from that fake pleasant to actual surprise. His eyes cast to mine and my heart almost explodes when his face softens. There's my baby. I missed him.

"Uh, yeah. I'm okay with that. Akmal, can we tag along?"

"You know you're basically family, Mat. Of course you guys are invited. My mother would be elated to have you over."

Atsuko must feel the same tension in the air that I do because after looking back and forth between Akmal and I, she quickly goes to Mat and grabs his hand.

"Alright! We'll see you guys tomorrow then!" She starts waving goodbye and Mat follows her out the front door, only giving Akmal a head flick as a goodbye.

I start walking towards Akmal as he locks the door behind our guests. When he turns, I bury my face into his chest and hug him. I don't know what's bothering him, and at first I was mad but now I just want him to be happy again.

It probably sounds like a mumble, but I speak into his chest anyway. "Akmal, what's wrong?"

At my question, he finally lets go of some of the tension he's holding and hugs me back. I like this. This feels right.

Lifting my head, I stare at his eyes to see if he still looks upset.

"I'm fine, now that I'm home." He releases me quicker than I'd like and walks towards the fridge to grab a bottle of water. He says he's fine, but why doesn't it feel that way?

"Talk to me. Why does it feel weird? Why have you been acting weird all day? Is it something I did?"

After a few gulps of water, Akmal turns to me and places the bottle on the counter. "What do you mean?" There's that fake smile again.

"Don't lie to me, Akmal. I don't know what's going on with you but you can't fool me with your 'everything's fine' smiles. Talk to me."

Running his hand through his hair, he lets out an exasperated sigh. Damn, what is that about?

"I don't know, Vero. I don't know what I'm doing, I've never been in a relationship. I feel like I'm in over my head with you because I can't get you out of my damn mind and every man that looks your way makes me feel less than a person. You could have any guy out there, *any*...why me, Vero? Am I something you just wanted to conquer? I feel like you're with me because you pity me. I don't know. You're the first girl who's made me feel this way, and I'm so damn confused all the time!"

"Why would you feel less than a person? You're the one I said yes to. We're getting married, doesn't that tell you my level of commitment to this, to us? No, I'm not with you because I pity you. Ain't nobody got time for that mess. I'm with you because I want YOU."

"I just - I just can't wrap my head around someone like you wanting someone like me. Then I come home and you're talking about dildos with Atsuko. I know you have more experience than me, I know you have needs that I just can't fix because of my culture. It frustrates me and at the same time I'm pissed you have to rely on a fake dick to take care of your needs. *I* should be the one to take care of your needs. ME. Just me. Nothing and no one else!"

Woah. I never realized something like a dildo would make Akmal feel so strongly. I mean, I get what he's saying, but damn.

Taking a tentative step towards him, I feel like I'm approaching a tiger pacing in a cage, ready to snap someone's head off. I've never seen this side of Akmal before. Keeping my voice calm, I try to reassure him again.

"Akmal...I don't want anyone else. If you don't want me to use a dildo, I won't. It's not a big deal."

"Not a big deal? Not a big deal? Vero, how can I even feel like a man when my future wife has to rely on something else to make her happy? It should be my job...no, *my* damn privilege to make my fucking woman happy in all ways. This damn time frame for this wedding is killing me because you're all I ever think about. From the moment I wake up, seeing you walking around this place, smelling your scent that's seeped into my clothes and the furniture. I'm struggling, Vero. I'm fucking struggling and you have no idea."

"Akmal, I don't know what to say. What do you want me to do? What can I do?"

"That's just it! There's nothing we *can* do until we get married and that day seems like a million miles away when my dick and heart is being pulled towards you every waking moment. Seeing guys look at what's mine with desire in their eyes *kills me.* It kills me, knowing that any one of them can give you what you need while I'm restricted! I'm trying damn hard to honor my family and I'm trying *damn hard* to find a middle ground to keep my woman happy. You don't think I see how much you need satisfaction? You don't think I see the need in your eyes when you look at me? I don't know what I'm doing, and it only emphasizes the fact that you probably deserve someone better than me."

What? No! I'm sad, I'm heartbroken, and you know what? I'm kind of pissed.

"Jode esto! No hables mal de ti ni de mi hombre."

"I don't understand what you're saying."

"I fucking said: don't be talking shit about MY man like that."

Akmal leaves the kitchen and walks away from me. Fuck no, we're not done talking. He doesn't get to walk away from me after spewing that kind of shit about the man I'm going to marry.

"Don't fucking walk away from me, Akmal."

He turns in anger and throws his hands out to the side. "This is me, Vero. The insecure virgin who doesn't know what the hell he's doing. You're too much woman for me. There, I admit it. If you want to leave, do it now because what you see is all you're going to get."

What the hell is wrong with him today? He's fucking making me pissed with all this shit spewing out of his beautiful lips.

Now *I'm* feeling irrationally angry because I just told him that I wanted him and yet he continues this self-deprecating behavior. Has someone told him this? Is this something on a deeper level?

He's walking backward as I walk forward. Hell no, he ain't getting away from this conversation that easily. The moment he's in front of the arm of the couch, I shove him, toppling his back onto the cushions. Climbing over him, I grab the front of his shirt and force his lips on mine. Since he's not going to fucking listen to my words, he's going to have to listen to my body. I'm tired of hearing his shit anyway. The time for talking is done.

He doesn't kiss back for a few seconds but after rubbing the palm of my hand against his neck and my fingers up to his hair, Akmal's lips surrender and he's giving it back to me with just as much passion. I lean into him, rubbing my breasts against his warm chest and he growls against me, the vibrations on my lips making my pussy clench. When his hand grips the back of my neck to pull me closer, I whimper into his mouth.

There's a storm of emotions brewing behind this complicated man of mine and it wants to suck me into the chaos. His hips grind up against me as his hands travel down to the small of my back, keeping me firmly against him like he's afraid I'll be the one to pull away. *Not going to happen.* The need surging through him is affecting me, making my own need grow exponentially. We're fighting fire with fire, making this tension between us grow into an inferno.

On one particularly hard grind, I let out a squeak as his hardness presses right against my clit, sending a spike of pleasure through me. This dress is thin and my senses are heightened with how much Akmal is devouring my mouth right now. He's actually the first one to push his tongue past my lips as I gasp on another hard grind. *My god, who is this man?*

My legs resituate themselves over his body to allow me to straddle him more comfortably as our mouths and tongues continue to fight. Fight for what, I don't know. Is it dominance? Is it something else altogether? I nip his bottom lip, making him groan as he kisses across my jaw, sending his own trail of nips down a path towards the crook of my neck. Shit, I'm so hot right now and so damn horny for this man. He's such a fast learner and it makes my pussy weep in anticipation.

My hand slips under the top of his jeans. This shit is fucking too tight for my liking. Without removing my mouth from his, my fingers deftly undo his button and fly to give my hands more freedom to play. Running my palm across his happy trail, I get a firm grip on his cock and start to play. It's hot, it's hard, and it is fucking weeping. This man is so damn sexy and he doesn't even know it.

Akmal is still kissing me feverishly as his hand comes back up to grip my hair, pulling it back to look me in the eyes with the most intense and vulnerable stare. "We can't do this." The fucker then kisses me again and makes me lose my damn mind with his intensity. "We shouldn't." Lips slamming into mine again, he makes my head spin with this push and pull. He needs to make up his damn mind!

Fuck this, we can find a middle ground. We don't have to stick it in, much to my pussy's dismay. I just need this man to let go of his frustrations. I can do that for him. I can make him feel good.

My hand starts to stroke his cock up and down faster as he groans into the crook of my neck. When his hands tentatively caress the side of my boobs, I almost mewl like a damn cat in heat and arch my body. Yes, I am *that* sex starved, I realize, but Akmal drives me crazy. I love and I hate it. But I love watching Akmal bloom in his confidence, especially after everything that came out of his mouth earlier. I can be that for him. I can lift him up to where he needs to be.

"I love it when you touch me."

"You're so damn soft. Fuck, you're going to kill me." I can feel his cock growing in size and I know he's close, making me even more excited and hot for him.

My kisses travel down his jaw before I whisper in his ear, "Do you want to cum in my mouth, Akmal?"

"Shit" is all I hear before he climaxes into my hand and between us. He crosses his arms over his face and groans again as his hips continue to thrust into my grip, sending spurts of cum between our bodies and clothes. I don't want him to feel bad about what happened or, heaven forbid, guilty. I just wanted to do something for him, to take away the tension of today. He deserves it. I wish I could do more but like he said, we can't.

Pushing his arm away from his face just enough to expose his lips, my mouth finds his once more as we kiss each other slowly, exploring the way our tongues touch and swipe one another without the frenzy of high-tense emotions.

Between our lips sliding against each other, Akmal keeps saying, "We shouldn't have done that." This poor boy and his inner conflict is going to drive me up the wall. I don't know how to respond to these types of statements. Despite his words, his body is telling me something completely opposite. It's relaxed, and his hands are caressing over my ass as we continue to make love with our mouths like we don't have a care in the world.

Chapter Nine

AKMAL

I don't know what happened to me. I was so pissed at all the men checking out Vero that my head wanted to explode. I'm not a violent person, but fuck if I didn't feel like stabbing the eyes out of every man that looked her way, and there were numerous. My emotions are all over the place and it scares me. I didn't know how to handle it, so I called up Mat to see if he could help me.

His solution was to go to the MMA gym with him. I've seen Mat at his lowest, and he was able to get himself out of it. I figured he'd be the best person to go to.

Taking out my frustrations on the heavy bag helped a little, but didn't fix the problem entirely. I was still pissed and I didn't know why. After showering at the gym, we came straight back to my place. The moment I opened the door was the moment the word 'dildo' filtered through, and it felt like my heart was being sliced through by a giant knife and twisted for maximum impact.

These aren't things I ever thought I would feel. The irrational anger and jealousy towards a damn dildo. I didn't even know she had one with the things she brought over, but I should have known. A woman like her needs sex, lots of it. She's walking sex on a stick.

My mind is so overloaded that I barely register Mat and Atsuko saying their goodbyes and leaving. My body was moving on autopilot as it closed and locked the door, only to be shocked back into the present when Vero hugs me. My chest aches like I can still feel the metaphorical knife continually being twisted, twisting my mind into thoughts I shouldn't be having.

It's not her fault she's so damn attractive. It's not her fault she's stuck with a guy like me. I shouldn't be selfish to want to tie her down to a guy like me.

The crap coming out of my mouth, once it started, kept flowing like uncontrollable vomit. It felt both good to get it out and scary because she might just believe the shit I'm saying and leave me high and dry.

Damn, just thinking about her walking out this door to another man's arms makes me boil with rage. Why am I so damn angry all the time?

Vero and I keep having slip ups and I can't say if I'm pleased or upset by the fact. My cock tells me he's more pleased than upset, that's for sure. We can't keep doing this. I need to stay away from her, regain some sort of control.

The living room incident feels like it was hours ago as well as only a few minutes ago. I can still feel the way her soft hands stroked against my erection, bringing me to heights I've never known. Dammit! I need to stop thinking about it.

Night has fallen and the house is dark and quiet. Quiet except for my thoughts as I lay here in the dark staring at nothing and wondering how I got myself into this. I don't regret asking her to marry me at all...but will I be enough for her? For a woman who can command a room by just bending over to look at some dresses. I don't even remember what she ended up buying because I was so preoccupied with rushing her out of that shopping center to bring her back home for safe keeping.

Turning onto my back, I run both of my hands down my face and try to stamp down these self-deprecating thoughts. Vero's right, I shouldn't do this to myself. I shouldn't think these things. The bed suddenly dips, startling me out of my mood. It's still dark in my room but I would recognize her scent anywhere. My cock is already twitching at the thought of her breasts and hands. Damn, will it always be like this between us?

"What are you doing?" Do I really want to know?

"I missed you." Her hand slowly skates across my naked chest and I can feel the goosebumps rising on my skin. "I'm tired of sleeping alone, Akmal. We don't have to do anything. Just...just let me hold you."

Okay, I can do that. That's not so bad.

My hand goes over hers as our fingers interlace. The bed jostles again as she moves her body even closer to my side, laying her head on top of my shoulder. This is new. This is nice. Her warmth suffuses into my skin like a blanket. I can get used to this. Is this what married people do everyday?

"Akmal, tell me your dreams."

"My dreams?"

"Yeah, what do you want to do in life? Was photography always your goal?" The thought of this woman wanting to get to know me, just me, makes my heart swell.

"Yeah, I guess so. It started as a hobby, and it's something I'm good at, I think. IT work forced me into a nine-to-five position and it felt so stifling. Photography lets me be my own man, making my own rules."

"I like that. You are good at what you do."

"Thanks. How about you? What are your dreams?"

"I love photography too, just on the other side of the camera. Atsuko and I both were trying to get modeling to be our full time gig so we wouldn't be restrained to our day jobs as well."

"What is your day job?"

"Oh, I guess it never got brought up, huh? I bartend at a local Cuban restaurant."

"Oh. Do you like it? Bartending, I mean."

"Yeah, I guess? It pays the bills. I guess I'm good at it since they haven't hired anyone else. They're pretty slow in the mornings, which is when I work. I took off after the Alfonso incident, so they're not expecting me back for a while."

"I'm glad you're off."

"Me too."

It becomes quiet after the conversation ends and my mind is going over everything she's told me. I wonder what kind of customers she gets when she's bartending? Are they rowdy? Is she safe? Is anyone there to look out for her?

Soon enough, her breathing starts to even out, lulling me into my own darkness.

I'M COMING OUT OF THE TAIL END OF A DREAM AND I'm getting frustrated. This is starting to become my constant state of being, it seems. Vero's face of ecstasy as she orgasmed is starting to fade like smoke in the wind the more the fog of sleep dissipates.

Burying my face into the softness in front of me, the scent of my woman takes over my mind. Vero's in my bed...and it feels so damn right, even though she shouldn't be here. I must have slung my arm around her because it's currently holding her like a damn teddy bear with her back pressed to my front. Her dark hair tickles my nose, making me move it towards the soft slope of her shoulder instead.

Some days I still can't believe she's real. I still can't believe she said yes to my stumbling proposal. How did I get so lucky?

My hands pull her in even closer towards my front in case this is all a dream and she really is going to disappear in front of my eyes. The moment my hard cock presses against her ass is the moment Vero starts to sluggishly squirm against me. No, this is not a dream. Not when I can feel the softness of her backside torturing me like that. How am I going to make it through today when we're like this? I can't seem to keep it down around her. I feel high strung from the pressure that's always between my legs, seeking relief where I know I'm forbidden to.

"Mmmm...." Damn, she sounds sexy in the morning. And now I'm thinking back to the tail end of that wet dream. Except she's real, she's here, and I'm holding her against me *right now*.

Would it be so bad? I can give her relief, right? She's always trying to give me relief, reading me like an open book when I'm strung so tight that I don't know what to do with myself. I've been selfish, I realize that now. What kind of husband am I? I need to do better but I don't know what the hell I'm doing half the time.

Trusting my gut, my hand starts to slowly run against her skin upwards under her top. She's so soft. When my fingertips graze across the underside of her breasts, my breath hitches. Shit, she's not wearing a bra. I can't stop now, can I? I'm too damn intrigued. We shouldn't. I'm going too far.

The moment my hand moves away is the moment Vero presses her ass against my crotch at the same time as she grabs my wandering hand and presses it fully over the entirety of her breast. *My god.*

Running my nose across her shoulder to the middle of her back, I'm glad she can't see how embarrassed I am with how much I want this.

Mumbling against her skin, I can feel her arch her back in response. "You're so fucking soft. What do you do to me, Vero?"

She forces my hand to squeeze her breast even harder and my hips start to move on their own, slowly thrusting against her. How do we keep finding ourselves in these compromised positions? How can any sane man say no to the temptation of heaven right in front of him?

"The same thing you do to me." The sound of her breathy voice in the morning is going to star in all my fantasies from here on out.

When her other hand guides mine between her legs, I groan against her skin, pressing a kiss to her back. Dammit, I'm so weak. I'm craving everything she's doing to me like my next breath. She pushes my fingers beneath her panties and they glide along the wetness that's already accumulating and soaking through her panties. *Fuck.*

"Tell me your fantasies, Akmal." Fucking hell, I can barely even think straight right now. How the hell am I supposed to answer that? She'll probably think I'm a pervert with everything I think about revolving around her.

"You don't want to know..."

I'm not in control of myself anymore as my fingers continue to explore her body, making her squirm and moan. It's just so damn wet and it makes me think of what it would feel like to shove my cock into its heat. Groaning against her back, I lick her skin slowly, just wanting her to be even more wet because of me. I can't believe I'm doing this. I can't believe she's this turned on.

"Tell me, Akmal. I'm so horny right now." I let out a conflicted groan. She can't say these kinds of things to me. Can I really deny such a simple request from my future wife? She just wants to know my mind. I can give her that. She needs to know me, the real me.

Her hands start to guide me higher, towards the top of her pussy where I can't see, but can feel a hood of skin peeking out. Taking her guidance and cues, I follow her silent commands and start to rub where she wants me to. Her moans become louder and it spurs me on. I think we're both chasing something as I continue to grind against her backside while my fingers circle her secret nub.

"I love how wet you are, it makes my dick want to cry with how much it wants to bury itself inside of you. Feel you from the inside."

Her breath hitches before she says, "Tell me more."

The air is starting to feel oppressed again with how hot it's getting. Kicking off the sheets to give us a little reprieve, my hand doesn't let up as it starts to stroke her pussy lips and bring the wetness up to her clit. I think that's what they call it.

"I can't stop thinking about the way your mouth takes my cock. The way it felt when I came and you took every drop. It's been the star of my fantasies every night, torturing me because I can't do a damn thing about it."

Knowing Vero, she never does anything halfway because she makes my free hand pinch her nipple under her shirt and I almost cum right there with the overload of sensations happening. My mind is stimulated to the point of no return, trying to decide which part of this moment I like the best. Fuck, I want it all. I want it all so bad. This wedding needs to hurry the fuck up.

"I love when you cum in my mouth, Akmal. I've been thinking about it every night too." Shit, she has? Fuck, it's so dirty. I love that she's dirty and is proud of it...and she's all damn mine.

"Are you a dirty girl, Vero?"

Her legs are scissoring at this point, pushing my hand even harder against her center. Damn, how can she get this wet? The thought of my dick plowing into this, sliding in and out and cumming inside of her makes me grit my teeth. I bet she tastes fucking good too. Didn't Mat talk about that? Licking pussy to put his woman into submission? The idea is sounding better by the minute. Fuck! We really shouldn't be doing this.

"I'll be anything you want me to be." God damn. What is she doing to me?

"I want to taste you so bad, but I know if I do, I won't be able to stop."

"Oh my god. I wish I could feel your tongue in my pussy. I'm so fucking wet for you, Akmal." Shit, the way she says my name at this moment, like I'm the most desirable person in existence for her. It makes me feel high, like I'm on top of the damn world.

Feeling braver, my fingers start to swirl against her clit and dip into her channel ever so slightly. Watching her reactions, my hand starts to play her the way her body is telling me to. She starts to pant, but so am I as I watch her body move like a damn siren song, calling me to my death.

"Oh my god, Akmal, don't stop." Hell no I'm not stopping, not when she looks like this. Almost exactly the way I remember from my dream.

Pinching her nipples and tugging, my other hand starts to rub her clit even harder when her body starts to jerk and she cries out in pleasure. Holy fucking shit, just look at her.

Suddenly, her hands seemed to have traveled between her legs to grab my cock from beneath my boxers somehow and she's sliding it against her pussy lips. Fuck!

She presses my shaft against her wetness while gripping the head of my cock, jacking me off between her legs. My breaths grow ragged and I almost see stars when it starts to spurt into her hands when my climax hits. How does it keep getting better with her? How can it possibly even feel better than the last times she's made me cum? Vero must be doing some witchcraft because I'm addicted. She's put a spell on me and I'm forever bound to this vixen who has me by the cock.

Her hand rubs against our combined juices right before she turns her head back to look at me and sticks her coated finger in her mouth.

I can't. I can't look at this and not fuck her right here. Biting her shoulder out of my frustration to make her stop her constant teasing, I jump out of bed right when she lets out a yelp. Serves her right. Damn her.

Jumping into the shower, I make sure to make the water as cold as it can go.

Chapter Ten

VERO

Despite the orgasm this morning, I'm a ball of nerves. I called up my familia and told them to be on time for lunch. Atsuko called me and told me they're already on their way.

Now I'm standing in this kitchen, staring at this chair where Akmal and I were last grinding on each other. How am I supposed to hold myself back at his parents' house? There is no possible way. I don't want to cause a rift between our families. I mean, I can't be all over him in front of my parents either. My mom would have my head while Fabian laughs his ass off.

Okay, I can do this. I need to prove to Akmal and his family that I'm in it to win it. I need to prove to Akmal that I'm committed to see this to the end. Taking a deep breath in and out, I close my eyes and try to find some sort of inner tranquility.

A throat clears behind me before I hear, "Are you ready?" Turning around, my eyes land on the most delectable sight. How can he be sexier every time I look at him? Is it because I'm starting to see him in a new light? Starting to unfold the many layers of Akmal? No matter what we've come across so far, I'm only more intrigued and determined to tie this man to me.

Akmal is standing there in dark dress pants and a very nice light blue button-down top which he has tucked neatly. *My my*. The color compliments his tan skin tone nicely. He almost looks out of my league, and that thought shakes my confidence a little. I watch as his hand starts to roll up his sleeves, one at a time, and I'm in a trance with his movements. What is it about a man with rolled up sleeves? Knowing exactly what those hands are capable of, my legs press together beneath my clothes.

My own hands smooth down the looser dress I'm in. It has a much higher neckline than I'm used to, channelling an Audrey Hepburn look, but at least it's loose-fitting enough to not have any mishaps with the girls. The flare of the skirt will also allow me to sit down easier when we eat on the floor.

"Vero, are you ready?" I was lost staring at the way the dress shirt stretched across his firm chest when his arms were moving around to make sure his shirt was nicely tucked in all the way. This wedding cannot come soon enough.

"Yes, I'm ready."

Leaving the apartment, Akmal opens the passenger door for me and I slide in before he comes around the other side. I'm a little nervous despite having met his parents already. Will they like my family? I really hope mi familia took my advice about dressing modestly. I was able to pre-warn them about eating on the floor and could hear Fabian yelling in the background about it being crazy.

I know. I know. This whole damn thing is crazy, but I wouldn't give up Akmal for anything. YOLO.

"Akmal, what should I be expecting? I'm assuming your mother is taking over all of the wedding planning? Will I be able to invite my relatives?" Last I remember, Akmal's mother already had an entire wedding list in mind.

"I honestly don't know. I mean, I never paid that much attention to it because...I never thought I'd find someone. I'm what Malaysians would consider old in regards to marriageable age."

"Okay...if you're old...what does that make *me*?" I'm older than he is! Does that make me a spinster?

He pulls up to the front of his parents house, places the car in park and turns to look at me. "It makes you mine."

Oh...be still my heart.

Once we step out of the car, Akmal places a hand behind the small of my back and I'm reminded of the day on the couch. Lord, don't get my lady bits going right before we meet his family. We're halfway up the walkway when I hear the rumble of Fabian's Chevelle pull up next to our vehicle. I can't believe he drove our parents in that thing.

They probably all smell like exhaust fumes. Akmal and I have stopped walking to watch as they get out.

My mother is in a long sleeve modest top with pants. My father is in his signature button-down short sleeve top and cotton pants. Fabian...well, good enough. Either his grey t-shirt shrank a little or his body has gotten larger because it's stretching across his pecs, not hiding much of what's underneath. At least his dark pants don't have any holes or stains on them.

"I look fine, quit judging, Vero." Dammit, I have a feeling something is going to go wrong today. My brother isn't the most well-behaved on good days. He didn't even bother to shave, leaving his five o' clock shadow on like it's a damn signature when in reality, he just doesn't want to be bothered by an extra step.

"Keep your trap filtered today, Fabian, I'm serio. Don't cause any trouble for me. I want this lunch to go well."

Fabian shoots his steel-grey eyes at me and I know there's going to be trouble. These virgin Malaysian girls don't stand a chance against his bad boy looks. His tattoo is peeking out a little from his short sleeve but it can't be helped now.

"What do you take me for? I'm going to be good, trust me." Famous last words coming from his mouth. I love my brother but he throws off an aura of trouble that most women can't say no to.

"I'm serious, Fabian."

Fabian smiles and I can feel my hands starting to get clammy.

"Relájate. Just relax."

"He's right. Relájate, Vero. It will be okay." My dad, always backing up my bro like it's some bro code. Traitor.

"Akmal, good to see you again." At least my dad is being civil this time.

"Yes, it's good to see you again as well. I hope the trip was okay?"

"Fabian was driving, we just sit until we get where we need to go."

"Well, thank you again for joining us. I'm sure my family is excited to meet you."

Akmal hasn't even finished his sentence yet when we hear the sound of his mother's voice. "There you are Akmal! What are you doing keeping everyone outside huh? Come, come! The food is ready. Mat is already here with his wife. Akmal, you didn't tell me he's already engaged! We need to make a double wedding huh."

We make it to the door where Akmal's mother is practically preening at the party coming in. After short greetings and everyone remembering to remove their shoes, we enter the living area where a large spread is already laid out.

"Vero!" Turning towards the sound of my name being called I see Atsuko making her way around the small crowd.

"Atsuko! When did you guys make it here?"

"Oh, only about ten minutes before you guys. Akmal's mother was basically all over Mat and how he didn't mention anything about me. They really do treat him like he's family. It's cute."

"Have you met the sisters yet?"

"I think I see them around the house getting things ready but I haven't talked to any of them yet." My eyes start looking around when I catch Akmal's first sister walking by.

"Hasanah!" Her head is covered in a light purple headscarf - or hijab, as google has informed me recently - as she turns my way.

"Ah! Sister, so glad to see you!"

I can feel Atsuko tense up next to me a bit. It's so subtle but being her BFF, I can read her really well. Atsuko came to this lunch in something similar to myself, a looser fitting, flared, vintage inspired dress with an appropriately sized cardigan top.

"How are you?"

"I'm good! Have you met Mat's fiancé, Atsuko?"

"Oh! So nice to meet you! I'm so happy for Mat, and for you of course. Now my mother can stop pestering me about marrying him."

"Oh...thank you. Yes, Mat and I are engaged."

"It is good, yes? Mat deserves the best. He is a great guy. He looks very happy with you. Congratulations."

The air between the two starts to thin out to friendlier terms. I knew Hasanah was a nice girl. Just a girl who got caught up with somewhat overbearing parents.

"Hidaya! Sakinah! Come! Meet Mat's wife." The other two sisters come towards us through the crowd and I notice a really big difference between the two. One girl looks to be wearing more modern and form-fitting clothing while the other dons what I assume is more traditional Malaysian clothing.

"This is Sakinah, she is twenty-five. I am the oldest, at twenty-six. Hidaya is twenty-three."

Sakinah does a little bow. Her dress is long sleeved but flows over her small frame nicely like a damn modern day princess while her younger sister wears a more traditional top and bottom skirt that matches in color with embroidery. Sakinah's hijab is a solid black, making it almost look like it's part of her dark hair. Very stylish.

"Nice to meet you. Glad my family didn't scare you off, Vero. Akmal deserves a strong woman to go up against all this." Sakinah and I share a knowing smile because I totally understand what she's saying. The clash of cultures can be a bit much. Overbearing parents, even more so.

"This is Hidaya, my youngest sister." This sister is in a soft pink hijab that makes her look very young.

"Hello, Vero. Nice to see you again."

"Thanks. Nice to see you too. This is my best friend, Atsuko. She is engaged to Mat."

Both the girls look at her with a smile, greeting her with a little bow. No one looks threatening or looks like they have any ulterior motives. Atsuko noticeably relaxes as she greets them back.

"Vero, don't forget about tu hermano. Introduce me." Awww shit. I know that look. Fabian's eyes are practically sparkling as they look at...who was she again? The middle sister, Sakinah.

What is this? It's so subtle but my woman's intuition catches it. Both Atsuko and I look at each other subtly. She catches it too.

"Fabian, these are Akmal's *sisters*. This is Hasanah, Sakinah and Hidaya." Look at this fool right here. He hasn't heard half of the introduction because he only has eyes for the princess in the middle.

Being the freaking Rico Suave he is, he grabs Sakinah's hand and bends down to kiss the back of it. How fucking embarrassing. I can already feel trouble radiating off him.

"Sakinah. What a beautiful name for a beautiful woman. I'm Fabian." Look at this guy right here. Her smile is so coy I want to vomit in my mouth. She's not really falling for this ish, is she? What the hell is happening here? Oh my god. Look at that smile on her face. She *is* falling for his crap. I can't blame her, she's probably never seen the likes of Fabian Hernandez in her life. Lord have mercy on her.

"Fabian. Akmal's sisters are good girls and need to stay that way." Aww crap, the smile that starts creeping up on his face shows his one dimple and I should have known I shouldn't mention the words 'good girls' because a guy like Fabian will take that as a challenge. I try to send Sakinah a look of warning but she only has googly eyes for Fabian since he hasn't let go of her hand yet.

Saving them from a potential scandal, I bump my body between them to break their contact and push Fabian towards my parents.

This fucker is still winking and blowing kisses over my shoulder at Sakinah as she giggles and walks away with her sisters in tow. He needs to rein that junk in before her parents catch him.

Akmal's parents usher us all to the floor to sit down and eat. It seems the parents have their own little circle while the rest of us have ours. The couples are sitting together, not too far from where the parents are, while somehow Fabian and Sakinah are sitting next to each other. What a coincidence, hey?

The food is delicious, as usual. I can hear the parents talking about wedding details while I'm trying to keep an eye on my brother to make sure his hands aren't straying where they shouldn't. Sakinah is just soaking up all the looks he's shooting her way, even if she isn't saying much. There's something about her. I might have to watch out for her too.

Once the meal is done, we all go to stand up while some of us start putting plates away. The front door crashes open and more voices are joining in from outside. I feel like this is deja vu.

"Aye Mat! You finally have a woman too! This is great news! We shall make it a double wedding huh. Tuah, bring the fabric! Zaka, where is Adila? We need to measure Mat's wife."

A whirlwind of people I don't recognize start coming in besides Akmal's aunts and uncles.

"Oye! Akmal, I was in the neighborhood and had to see if it was true. Where is your wife? Finally huh?" Who is this guy? He's got to be related to Akmal somehow. A random stranger or acquaintance wouldn't just waltz in, right?

A few more guys and what looks to be their partners come through the door and I'm feeling overwhelmed again. My parents are speaking to each other in Spanish and I have no idea where Fabian is.

Chapter Eleven

FABIAN

A bunch of people are popping in. This place is crazy. That or their family is huge. But you know what? It gives me the perfect opportunity to find out about this middle sister I've been recently introduced to. Maneuvering myself between all the moving parts currently happening around us, I catch sight of her black head wrap. I'm kind of glad she stands out in this sea of jewel-toned colors mingling back and forth.

I watch as she walks back and forth to what I think is the kitchen, putting plates away with the other girls. On one of her walks back into the living room, I whisper her name when she's close enough to hear.

"Sakinah." Her black headwrap whips around and I give her a smile. I watch as her cheeks pinken and I know I got her. She feels it too, this thing between us. Can't say I've ever run across a Malaysian girl, but they can't be that much different than other girls, right?

There's only one way to find out.

"Yes?"

"Can you direct me to your bathroom? I'm a little lost in this place with all these people around." In my periphery, I can see different women gathering together around my sister and her best friend. Bolts of fabric are being held overhead as people start chatting around us, creating a buzz in a sea of voices. I don't know how Vero handles all this shit. I would have been gone by now if it wasn't for this being Vero's day. I wouldn't want to embarrass her like that. I can be good.

"Yes, of course. Follow me." Making my way close behind her, I can see that she really isn't that tall, only standing to my chest. That's alright, I don't mind them being tiny. She smells like something floral, it's light and it's nice. Makes me want to lean in to get a better whiff. Watching the sway of her hips in her dress, I'm mesmerized by the flow of the movement. Why are all these women so covered in seas of fabric? Is this a Malaysian thing?

My mind is now imagining what lies underneath this dress of hers. Is she slender? Just a handful? Would her skin be as soft as silk since it's been kept from the sun, without a blemish in sight? How sensitive would she be to touch? Would she writhe with every breath I blow across her skin? Would she scream in pleasure as I lick her pussy?

My cock is already twitching at the thought of what it would feel like to cover her body with mine when she stops and turns to point at a door in front of me.

Her startled face is getting pink again as I stand in front of her about a couple feet away, staring at her to my heart's content, looking over every detail and memorizing it. I'm sure everyone in the other room is busy with whatever they're doing. They wouldn't notice us missing for a while. Does it make me a bastard for thinking this way?

Her face has the most beautiful even tan coloring and it makes my mouth water for a taste. I wonder if she'd let me?

Vero's words come back to my mind about Akmal's sisters being 'good girls'. *That's what they all say*. I've been with plenty of 'good girls' who ended up being more promiscuous than I am. They were just better at hiding it from their families.

Speaking of sex, I haven't had some for a while with work getting busy. But this little thing in front of me might just be what breaks my fast.

Sakinah's lashes lower and I'm intrigued. Is she shy? What is she hiding? Is she really a 'good girl' as they say? If so, then why was she so willing to lead me to the restroom without anyone else the wiser. I am a man after all, and she's a woman. Is it a subliminal invitation?

I'm a little upset that she doesn't want to look at me right now. There's no one else here but us. I know I'm not bad on the eyes. Grabbing her chin with my fingers, I force her face up to look at me and offer her another smile to calm her nerves. Her brown eyes sparkle with something behind them, but it's when her full lips part that I throw everything out the window and go in for the kill. Who could blame me? She looks like a damn offering.

She tries to escape by walking backward, only succeeding in trapping herself against the wall. *All part of the plan, baby, all part of the plan.* I take it easy on her, since it seems like she's unsure. *Or maybe this is her first time?* That thought does something to me. I've never been with a virgin before, and she sure is acting like what I think one would. Well, this is something new. It's making me even more hungry for her.

Brushing our lips together in the most chaste manner I can muster, I let my lips linger against hers for just a bit longer than I should without coaxing anything else. Her body tenses up but she doesn't slap me, so this is a good start between us. Her lips are definitely as soft as they look. When I pull back slowly, my eyes scan hers to make sure I didn't traumatize her.

Well look at that. Her eyes can't stay on mine for more than a few seconds since they keep going back to my lips. Things just got much more interesting.

"Why did you do that?" She bites the bottom of her lip and I internal high five myself for being able to bait the little thing so easily.

"Why not?"

"Because we shouldn't." Is that so? Her eyes go a little wild before she shoves me off her and slips away back into the crowd. So she does have a little fire in her after all, not as submissive as I thought. Now I'm hungry to find out more.

Sakinah, Sakinah, Sakinah. She's probably too young for me but fuck it. I'm not stopping until I get this one under me.

I should use the restroom to make it look legit before I rejoin the others as well. Laughing to myself, I open the bathroom door and start planning ways to catch myself a pretty little Malaysian princess.

AKMAL

The women are surrounding Vero and Atsuko with all their craziness, leaving the men to the side. Mat is chilling next to me when one of my cousins starts his bullshit that I'm quite frankly tired of hearing after all these years. He needs to find a damn new hobby.

"Took you long enough to find a woman." Uncle Zaka's son, Umar, has been one of the worst ones hounding me about this. Just because he was the first to get married out of our group, he always acts like that makes him a little better than us. Well, mostly better than *me*.

"I never thought you would, you know? I would have introduced you to my wife's friend from the university if you would have just said yes." Cousin Ismail hounds me too, but he's nicer about it. I understand everyone's concern. I shouldn't have stayed single this long.

Glancing over my shoulder, I watch as Vero laughs about something the girls are talking about. The reason I've stayed single this long is because the perfect woman was waiting for me to come into her life. She's the only one I can see myself with. I regret nothing.

"How did you even get a woman like that to want you huh? You don't have much to offer her." He's just lucky we're related. Doesn't he realize I already know all this? I ask myself that every damn day I'm with her.

I'm tired of this conversation already and it's only started.

"Don't let it get to you man." My buddy Mat is mumbling under his breath next to me, and he's right. I can't let all this negativity get to me.

Looking over my shoulder again to make sure Vero is alright, I spot Sakinah coming from the back to join Hidaya in the kitchen. When my eyes catch Fabian coming from the same direction shortly after, my mind is rewinding what Sakinah looked like when she came out. She looked okay, nothing seemed out of place. But why would they both be coming from the same direction around the same time?

I don't have time to ponder the thought when I see something that makes me see red. Umar's brother, Nosiah, is approaching my woman and I have a feeling I won't like what he has to say.

I'm barely registering what Umar or Ismail are talking about, when my ears start to strain to hear what's about to happen.

"Hey beautiful. If you ever get tired of Akmal, just know I'm here to catch you when you fall. I'm Nosiah."

My sisters are laughing but my mind can only see my fist in my cousin's face. My legs have already started walking towards Vero before he even opened his mouth. Lucky for him, my fist was only coming up halfway when my mother slaps him upside the head.

"Be respectful, huh? What are you doing? This is Akmal's wife. Look elsewhere for your own. If I hear something else coming from your mouth like that, you won't have a voice left after I beat you." Nosiah has the decency to look sheepish as he walks away, but not before I snarl at him and hit him upside the head a second time when he's close enough.

I know she's fucking beautiful. It doesn't mean they can try to steal her right from underneath my nose.

Nosiah continues to rub his head as he heads towards the other men. When I turn around to look at Vero, she is staring right at me with an expression I can't read but it makes my chest feel full. The smile she sends my way makes me think of nights holding her as she falls asleep in my arms.

Vero is mine, and I'm going to make sure she doesn't escape before the wedding gets here.

"Akmal, there you are. Give this ring to your wife, huh. That way the other boys will see she is already taken." My mom's got my back. She's right, I need to claim her in front of my cousins before one of the other boys get any ideas.

The second the piece is placed in my hand, I quickly stride the rest of the way towards my future wife. She startles at my arrival but quickly relaxes and her smile widens at me, making her face even more radiant as I grab her right hand and slowly place the engagement ring on her finger.

It doesn't matter what it looks like as time stands still between us. Our eyes make promises to each other as we try to restrain ourselves from public affection in front of our families.

Soon. Very soon, I'll be able to claim her in all ways.

"Daughter, the wedding will be ready by the weekend, huh. So get plenty of sleep so that you can look beautiful on the throne."

The smile that graces both our faces in that moment, tells her that the day cannot come soon enough.

Chapter Twelve

VERO

Yesterday was insane. It went from a casual lunch date to planning two weddings. At least my parents were able to add some input into the guest list. We're probably in the thousands by now and that thought scares me. How can there be that many Malaysian people in this one area? I swear Akmal is the first Malaysian I've ever come across and suddenly they're all coming out of the woodwork.

My fingers start to play with my engagement ring as my thoughts come back to the situation at hand. I need to pick up my paycheck from the restaurant. My boss was kind enough to give me a quick call earlier to let me know it's waiting for me.

"Akmal, can you drive me to my work so I can pick up my paycheck? I want to deposit it today since we're free."

"Yeah, of course."

I watch Akmal walk to the kitchen to pick up his car keys and I'm getting kind of flustered. I love the way his body moves against his t-shirt. The way his forearms look when they flex and grab the keys. When he turns to me, the slight facial hair he has makes me imagine what it would be like to feel it between my legs. He came in and left the shower that one day so quickly, I didn't get a chance to check out his tan body but now I'm so curious. His skin is so damn smooth, now it reminds me of how smoothly his fingers were playing with my pussy the other morning.

And last night...

"Hey, let's go online tonight. Join me?"

"Of course. Do I get to sit on your lap Akmal?" He chokes on his drink and takes a moment to clear his throat. I love doing that to him. He acts like he doesn't like my unfiltered mouth, but he loves that shit.

"Vero..." I pout at him before I let out an exasperated sigh and sit to the side of him rather than on him like I wanted.

We're on the floor with two laptops on the coffee table with our backs to the couch. Akmal is such a nerd with his gaming, but I love it. I've been trying to get into it with him so we can have something else to share together.

The game starts and soon enough, Akmal is so engrossed in what he's doing, he doesn't notice me scooting a little closer.

I'm almost in front of his laptop screen, but he's too lost in his raid. A few more butt scooches and I'm leaning in to breathe against his ear right before I lick his earlobe.

"Shit."

I'm laughing on the inside, but I'm not letting up. Not when he's being so cute.

I can see his character die in my periphery. Poor baby. Placing my palm on his cheek, I force his face towards me and kiss him deeply. My tongue is licking the seam of his lips asking for entry, and Akmal doesn't disappoint when he turns to me completely to devour my mouth. He's gotten too good at this lately, and my pussy is curious to see how well he takes instructions down there.

Pulling him with me as I lay myself down onto my back, Akmal follows without much resistance. Yeah, he feels it too. Our mental walls are getting thinner the more we try to fight this growing need for each other.

I don't know what happens, but suddenly Akmal growls and is kissing the crook of my neck as one of his hands pulls down my off-the-shoulder top, revealing one of my naked breasts to him.

I'm lost in the moment, panting at how worked up he's gotten me, when Akmal's lips go from my neck to swiping his hot and wet tongue over my nipple... and leaves me in a trance on the floor while he goes back to his original position and respawns his character.

"Wha-" I blink a few times, unsure how I got here. My brain is slow in leaving the lust fog. My nipple is getting

hard from the chill in the air, reacting to the wetness he left behind.

Seems I'm not the only one who's learned the art of the tease.

I don't know if I'll make it to our wedding day. I'm just going to stop lying to myself. How can he be so strong? I'm so weak, so weak for this man.

"What?"

"You make me so fucking horny."

He groans, turns away from me and runs his hands through his hair in frustration. I'm watching the way his back flexes with the movement, almost panting. I know I don't make it any easier, but dammit it's the truth! Being on the pill should curb your libido but I swear it does *nothing* for me! The last time I picked up my prescription for pills, I was told it got rebranded or something. How long ago was that? I don't remember but shouldn't the pill make your horny-chemical go down? I swear I've been nothing but horny since Akmal came into my life. I can't even think straight and find the right words in my mind.

Oh my god, what if it's because I haven't been doing it? What if there is some sort of build up inside of me that makes it worse? What should I do? I can't use a dildo after our last argument. I don't want Akmal to feel less than what he is.

Akmal is taking deep breaths before he turns around to look at me with the horniest eyes I've ever seen on him. This fucker isn't helping anything!

"Vero, you can't say that kind of stuff to me. I'm trying really hard here."

"I like you hard." Shit, I swear it just came out of my mouth. Oh my god, I want him to cum in my mouth again.

"Dammit Vero! I'm dying here."

"Maybe..maybe I can help you?" His eyes are intensely staring a hole into me. I'm not sure if I should be scared, but it's pulling me in like a fish hook. My legs are already moving by themselves until I'm standing in front of him. His arms are still up with his fingers threaded through his hair.

Don't make this so easy for me.

Shit, too late.

Taking one more step closer, my hands creep under his shirt and go across his abs as Akmal throws his head back and closes his eyes with a frown.

"You feel so good. I just want to make you feel good."

His voice is so gravelly, my vagina is screaming at me to claim what's rightfully mine.

"Vero...We can't do this. Stop."

I pout. Dammit! I want him!

When he opens his eyes and brings his head down, his frown turns into a delicious masculine chuckle as his warm hands hold my face to bring it in for a soft kiss. A teasing kiss. A kiss that's killing me.

"Akmal, let me suck you. I'll be quick. I just want you in my mouth so bad."

"Dammit Vero. Stop. Let's go get your paycheck, okay? This apartment is nothing but a box of temptation. We need to stop before we can't." Even the way he's saying all this against my lips, as we continue to give each other soft kisses, is killing me from how sexy it is.

My nails start to scrape his sides as they travel to his back, pulling him in closer to me. He growls into my mouth when my nails dig in again but manages to push me away, the bastard!

He's panting as he walks a few steps away from me. I'm panting from the way he's leaving me.

After a few moments of silence and separation, Akmal sighs and turns towards me enough to lace his fingers into mine as he pulls us out the front door to the apartment. The tension between us is palpable. You can almost feel the energy spike when our skin touches.

The drive over to Havana Palace was a quiet one. I still feel a little frustrated with what happened before our exit. Akmal shouldn't look so damn hot in the driver seat, flexing his arms as he works the steering wheel the way he does. Would his arms look like that when he's above me, plowing into my pussy until I cry out in ecstasy?

I'm pulled from my reverie when he puts the car into park and looks at me expectantly. Sighing, I lean my head back and breathe deeply a few times. It's getting harder and harder being around him like this. Wanting yet unable to take.

I still love him being around me despite the torture it brings.

“Akmal, will you come in with me please?”

“Of course, whatever you want.” I groan at that statement.

“Akmal you know what I want. But all I can have right now is you beside me.”

“Vero, it won't always be like this.” He’s already exiting the driver side as I answer him anyway.

“...I know...”

Once he opens the door for me, we walk hand in hand to the Cuban restaurant. It’s still slow in the morning, so I’m sure the manager doesn’t mind me bringing Akmal in with me to pick up this damn paycheck.

Mike, my boss, sees me and gives me a little wave before he heads back to his office. I’m showing Akmal around a bit before leading him to the bar stools to sit while we wait for Mike to get back. The front door of the restaurant opens up, but I don’t notice it as I lean in towards Akmal, imagining what it would have been like if we would have met in a place like this.

His chocolate eyes are staring into mine lovingly when I hear my name being called.

"Vero?"

That's not Mike's voice, but it sounds very familiar. Turning, I see a young guy that looks to be in his twenties with wavy brown hair. I know him from somewhere but I can't pinpoint where at the moment.

Giving him what I think is a friendly smile, I respond with a "Hi, do I know you?" Does that make me a bitch? I mean, he knew my name. But he could have just heard my boss calling me when I was behind the bar working some days too.

"You don't remember me? We met right here, in this restaurant." It's honestly still not ringing a bell. If I had a rendezvous with this guy, and by the way he keeps staring at my tits this is probably the case, he must have been a five pump chump. Not really worth me remembering.

Oh shit.

I turn my face to look at Akmal and his eyes are blazing but his face doesn't give anything away. He's so quiet that it kind of scares me.

Turning back quickly, I try to diffuse the situation. "Sorry, I honestly don't remember. But it was nice seeing you...again?"

When I catch his eye stray to my breasts again, it all happens so fast. By the time I realize what's happening, the poor guy is on the ground and Akmal still has his hand in a fist. He didn't even make a sound, how did he move so fast?

"Vero, take this and go. I'll clean this up. Shit, maybe it's good you're still off."

"Thanks Mike." Grabbing the check and sticking it into my purse, it almost doesn't make it all the way in when Akmal silently grabs my hand and pulls me out of the front doors and into the car.

The drive to the bank was silent. Instead of going inside, Akmal took us through the drive through ATM machine to deposit my check. I trust him so I gave him my card and number to put into the machine. He won't look at me the entire time he's performing his duties.

When we make it home, Akmal continues to be a gentleman with opening doors and such but the neverending silent treatment is making my head want to explode. I don't know what to do or say. I mean, that guy was before meeting Akmal. Should I feel sorry about it? But it wasn't like I planned to do the guy right before meeting Akmal. I didn't know I would fall for Akmal so hard.

"Akmal, what's wrong?" We've just come through the front door and he's walking directly to his bedroom.

Not knowing what else to do, I follow behind him ... only to see him packing a backpack. What the hell?

"Akmal, what are you doing?" Silence. His movements are jerky. He's pissed at me. I'm getting pissed too because I don't know why. I mean, I kind of do, but it's not my fault. I didn't do it TO him. How can I explain it when he won't even talk to me?

He turns to leave the room and I'm chasing right at his heels. Now I'm getting a little scared.

"Where are you going?"

The sound of the door slamming closed is the last thing I hear as my heart gets shredded into jagged pieces.

Chapter Thirteen

AKMAL

I'm being irrational, I know it. But that's the thing with irrationality, right? It makes no damn sense. Like how I feel right now. I feel like going back to that stupid restaurant to tear that fucker's head off but I know I shouldn't.

I feel like finding all of Vero's exes and killing them all, but I can't. And because I can't do these things my hands are itching to do, I inadvertently take it out on my wife. Fuck.

I had to leave. I couldn't be there anymore. I don't know what I would have ended up doing. Would I ever hurt Vero? Hell no. But I can't say the same for the shit that might come out of my mouth in the heat of my rolling emotions. I don't even know what I'm feeling, I just know I'm feeling A LOT.

This is all new for me. Apparently, this isn't all new for her and that thought spears me again in the damn chest. Fuck, I'm in over my head with this woman. She probably has a line of men waiting for her to come back to them. Here I am thinking I would be man enough to keep her?

Who thought I'd be this stupid?

I must have been brooding the whole way back to my parent's house. Pulling up to the front, I throw the car in park and get out with the small bag of clothes I packed. Was it immature of me? Probably? But it made sense at the time and I'm already here.

Walking up to the front door, something inside of me niggles at me, telling me I'm overreacting. I just need some time to think. Think about all this without her distracting me, tempting me. My parents still don't know we live together, which is a good thing. They won't know I left my wife alone in my apartment.

Knocking on the door, my mother opens it before I can get the second knock in.

"Eh? Why are you here Akmal? Is everything okay?" I don't think I have it in me to talk sensibly right now, so I slip in and throw my backpack on the ground right before I sit down on the couch with a frustrated groan.

"Akmal, where is your wife huh? Why are you here?" My mom isn't going to let up until I answer her.

"We got into a fight. I need some space to think." I mean, despite not really saying much to each other, it was kind of a fight, right? Ugh, why do I feel like shit just mentally saying that?

Everyone around me doesn't speak another word as they go about the rest of their day.

My mind is in a jumble. Vero has gotten under my skin and into my soul. Even if it was scraped out with serrated knives, she'd still be there. I always knew she was too good for me.

Fuck, is this love? Is this why this shit hurts so bad? I can't think straight. My chest feels constricted, like it's in a damn invisible vice grip. It hurts being away from her and right now, it hurts being next to her. What the hell am I supposed to do in a situation like this? Is there a damn manual to relationships I don't know about? Shit, even if there was, they've never seen the likes of Vero. She's one of a kind.

And now my sorry ass is fucking missing her and it hasn't even been that damn long. I can't go back to her like this though. Not in the state I'm in, like I'm fucking drowning without a life jacket.

The background noise starts to become a low buzz as I lay here on the couch, facing the back cushions.

I think I heard my name called a few times but I'm not sure if it was a dream. It sounds so muffled and my head feels heavy, weighed down by everything that's going on in my mind. Every time I close my eyes I see her face, the way she smiles when I look at her. The way her eyes seek me out in a room, the same way I seek hers, like magnets being pulled together. It makes my chest hurt even more. Fuck.

I must have fallen asleep on the couch because the feeling of someone sitting down next to me, jostling me, wakes me out of this zombified stupor I've found myself in.

"Ibu, don't kacau him. Leave him be."

"Move your legs huh? I want to watch my show and you are in the way." I scrunch up into more of a fetal position as the sound of the TV starts to pull me back into the darkness of my mind.

VERO

What just happened? What *just happened*?

He left me. Without a damn word. With a backpack of clothes slung over his shoulder. Is he coming back? Do I wait for him? What do I do?

This is why I was afraid to do this relationship shit! I can't handle this. I don't know the rules to play this damn game. I thought we were doing good. I thought we were making headway with how much we feel about each other.

Why am I feeling so fucking guilty, like my heart is dragging on the floor?

I can't even say sorry for whatever it is he's feeling because he's not even here.

My eyes suddenly feel really hot. I hate this shit. *Hate this shit*!

Flashbacks of my highschool sweetheart leaving me after he got what he wanted flash through my mind. The way I felt like my heart was being eviscerated and stomped on.

Akmal isn't like that though. I know he's not. But why does it hurt so damn much? I don't even know when my hands became fists at my chest until I feel wet drops on them. Fuck, I'm crying. *I hate this shit.* Once it starts, it doesn't stop.

I was fucking trying. I was trying... So. Damn. Hard. To be with him. Can't he see that? Can't he see my devotion? One fuck up. *One* fuck up.

Fuck, who am I kidding? I'm probably always going to fuck up. That fool isn't going to be the last to come out of the woodwork. And when it happens, will Akmal leave me everytime? Will it always be like this?

What if he doesn't even come back *this* time? What if I made the biggest mistake of my life by letting him leave?

I can feel my heart cracking at that thought. No no no no. He's it for me. I can't go back after this. There's not going to be anyone to live up to him. I'm ruined for all men.

The sob that tears from me is ugly and loud. I try to stifle it by covering my face with my hands but it only serves to make me cry harder, my body shaking from the hiccups. Dammit!

I need to move. I need to do something. But what? My feet somehow have led me to Akmal's room and I'm crawling into his bed, grabbing a shirt he left behind and sniffing it while crying on my side.

What the hell am I supposed to do?

Chapter Fourteen

AKMAL

Someone's pushing me, but my body feels sluggish. Shit, what day is it? I'm so damn tired, just a few more minutes.

This person isn't letting up and I'm starting to get a little pissed. I'm waving my hand outward haphazardly without opening my eyes when I get hit by something hard.

"Wake up! Allah, it's so messy in here. Wake up!" I get hit again and I finally open my eyes to blurrily see my mom with her hijab around her head and a wooden spoon in her hand. Shit.

"You need to wake up Akmal! I'm tired of watching you like a slug in the garden. You don't do anything but sleep. Wake up! Get out of this room!" It almost aches to move. Maybe she's right. I've probably been in one position for so long my body isn't used to moving anymore.

"I cannot even watch my shows when you are like this next to me on the couch huh! It ruins the mood. I want to enjoy the things I watch, not watch you like this."

My mom leaves my room after she pushes me one more time off the bed. Forcing myself into the restroom the shower helped a bit with getting my muscles warmed up and moving again.

Coming out of my childhood room turned into a guest room, I see everyone working on the wedding and I feel a pang in my chest again. Dammit, it hasn't gone down one bit. What if she doesn't even want me anymore?

"Walao eh. Oh my god, Akmal is still alive."

"Very funny Sakinah."

"Don't be rude la, Sakinah. You keep going to university then you find a good man to marry. Don't find one that makes problems like your brother." Am I the one making problems?

"Are you alright? What happened? Where is Vero?" Hasanah, ever the civil and calm one. How does she do it? This house is already getting to me.

"Hidaya! Make some rice huh!" Just another day for my mother it seems.

"I don't know. I'm sure she's okay." Am I sure?

"Haiyo, my son. You need to go fix this and make sure you marry her huh. We are almost done with the wedding plans already." Can I fix this? What if I messed it all up and the wedding gets canceled?

I can still see her face in my mind, the way her hands feel on my skin. The way she would hold me at night like it's the best thing in the world for her. Her smiles light up my fucking world every time she turns them to me. The way her beautiful lips would tilt up just the slightest when she's thinking of doing something she shouldn't.

How did I survive without those things? I guess the saying is right, you never know what you have until it's gone. Fuck, did I mess up?

A hand slaps the back of my head hard, knocking me out of my thoughts.

"Ow, what was that for?"

"For you being stupid right now. If you do not fix this you can move home and I will find someone for you to marry so this wedding does not go to waste. Then you can go to work with your bapa huh. I don't want a lazy son la."

"Walao eh." She slaps me upside the head again when she hears me say oh shit. Rubbing the back of my head, I think I just got the kick in the ass I needed to get me out of this stupor. I just got myself out of a constricting nine-to-five job, I don't want to be thrown into another.

And she's right. I am being stupid. I do need to fix this mess I created.

"Aye it's okay huh. Your bapa will not mind having you under his thumb at work. Less work for him." Ah crap. No. No no no no. I can already feel the metaphorical ball and chain being put on me with this conversation.

I fucking miss Vero. She's always been a breath of fresh air. The one to just ask me about me, the things that make me tick. Man, I've been stupid. How long have I been here?

"You've been here two days Akmal. I think it's time for you to go and fix this thing with your wife." Hasanah, reading my mind. Shit, two whole days? Where did the time go? I feel like I just fell asleep.

Rubbing my hand down my face as I sit on my parents' couch, I try to figure out the best way to approach this situation. Will she want me back? Will she be pissed?

...Is she even going to be there when I go back?

Fuck, the thought of her gone has me scrambling to grab my wallet and keys, running out the door.

VERO

There's no more ice cream in the house, and now I'm crying all over again. I'm still too embarrassed to call Atsuko and tell her of my failures. It was my fault, my past caught up with me and now I'm not even sure if I'm single or still engaged.

I tried calling Akmal a million times but it just goes straight to voicemail. Am I really that bad of a person, to not want to even talk to me?

I probably shouldn't be here. He probably wants me gone. He hasn't been home for two days and I'm still just as lost.

Do I go home? I don't have an apartment anymore. Where is there for me to go? I can't crash at Atsuko's place, three's a crowd and I don't think I can stand watching them happy together when my world is burned to the ground.

So here I am, crying all over Akmal's pillow again because it smells like him and I'm pathetic and miss the bastard like I've never missed anything before. To be honest, I think this heartbreak is exponentially worse than the one I had at eighteen. Fuck, I feel so low. I'm too much of a hot mess right now to even consider leaving the house.

What's the point of leaving anyway?

Dammit, I feel like I'm going in circles as my mind gets flushed into the realm of negativity. Closing my eyes, I can see Akmal's handsome face and the way he always looks out for me, making sure I'm alright. The way Akmal looks like we're both fighting this thing between us but wanting to give in anyway.

I miss him. It hurts.

It hurts *so fucking bad*. My sobs are getting louder again and no matter how hard I shove a fist at my chest, it doesn't dull the ache I feel. How can my heart feel like it's getting squeezed when no matter how hard I try, I can't scratch it out of me?

No one told me love was supposed to hurt like this.

The bed is shaking from my wracking sobs and this pillow is getting so damn wet. I should wash it, but then it wouldn't smell like him anymore.

Another loud sob escapes my lips without meaning to and suddenly I feel warm arms wrap around me tightly.

Now my mind is going insane. *It hurts.* Don't do this to me God. Don't play with me. I've lost everything already, don't let me lose my mind too.

When the feeling of facial scruff rubs against my neck, I open my eyes. My mind can't be that good and gone, can it?

Turning and hoping I don't see thin air, I take a harsh intake of breath when Akmal's face is right next to mine. At least I think it's him. My vision is too blurred by my tears.

Letting out another sob, I turn completely to bury my face against his chest and embrace him tightly in case he decides to leave me again. I can't. I just can't. If he leaves me again, I'm going to swear off all men and join a damn convent.

My pussy takes that moment to mentally slap me. Okay, I might be getting a little over dramatic but dammit!

"Ak-Akmal -" *hiccup* "Y-you came back to me. I'm so sorry!" I don't care whose fault it is, I just don't want to be apart anymore. I need him, I feel so lost without him.

"Shhh...shhh...I'm so sorry Vero. I was stupid. I was stupid." His arms band around me tighter at the same time mine does to him.

Look at us. I don't even know what the hell is going on anymore but it feels right to be in his arms again.

His hands cradle my face but I don't want him to see what a hot mess I am, so I bury myself deeper into his chest. Through the snot and the hiccups, I'm still able to take a deep breath in and smell Akmal as it seeps into my very pores.

I showered this morning but I'm sure he doesn't want to see me like this. But his hands are applying more force to bring my head up. Letting out a sigh, I submit to his request and when his eyes land on mine, I can feel fresh tears streaming down my cheeks.

"Vero, I'm sorry. I'm just... not used to feeling all of this."

"I'm sorry for making you feel like you had to leave me. I still want us to be together, Akmal. You're the only one I've ever wanted." I sound like a desperate and pathetic woman but I don't care. I *am* desperate for him. My mind is telling me to just say the words out loud. That it's probably the reason why he hasn't felt my devotion to this, to us.

I'm so scared.

"You didn't do anything wrong. I'm just...I don't know. I just know I can't live without you and the thought of you possibly leaving me for something better makes me want to claw my heart out. I don't think I could ever take it if it were to happen and so I ran, like the coward I am. I just didn't want to see you not wanting me anymore."

My fists are now punching his chest with this ludicrous line of thinking he's spewing at me! *You know why he feels this way, Vero. You never told him. Never reassured him.* I know! I know dammit, but the last time I told someone, it almost ruined me.

But look at me now, I'm already ruined, aren't I? My hands stop punching as I try to blink away the tears so I can see his face clearly. He looks just as vulnerable as I am, lying on his side, watching me with anticipation.

We're two peas in a fucking pod, both afraid the other is going to leave. How did we get here?

When his thumb brushes away my latest tear falling, I finally give myself the kick in the ass I needed.

"Akmal, I love you. You're the only one for me, don't ever think anything else." His thumb stops stroking and I can't read his expression. His breathing is becoming erratic, but so has mine. Please don't leave me hanging like this with my heart on my sleeve. Please don't crush it.

Akmal presses his forehead against mine and I close my eyes and brace myself for the rejection that I know is coming. I should have never pushed him these past few days. I should have never done that because now he's done with the frustration. He's done with me. I'm a hot mess. I'm making his peaceful life a hot mess.

"Vero, you've been the only one for me. I felt so deeply about stupid things and reacted like an idiot because...I'm stupidly in love with you. I can't even control myself around you. I can't even get a handle on my thoughts. My every waking dream is with you in it, don't ever think otherwise."

It takes a moment for his words to sink in, for the walls I've already started to build up to slowly be taken down again.

Did I just hear him correctly?

"You love me?"

When the feel of his lips reaches mine, I open my eyes to see him staring right back at me. It's a chaste kiss, but one that knocks me right in the gut.

"I love you, Vero."

I don't know who this woman is right now but I'm launching myself into Akmal's chest again as a fresh new wave of tears and sobs come out of me like someone fucking died.

I guess someone did die. The old me who would have never taken the chance, the old me who didn't want to put her heart out there anymore.

And you know what, I don't miss the old me because she didn't have Akmal.

I WAS SO MUCH OF A HOT MESS, AKMAL HAD USHERED me into the shower, telling me that he needed to wash the shirt I had on, the one he left behind on the bed. I didn't smell that bad, I mean... well, I didn't wash the shirt for two days because I wanted it to smell like him.

After a hot shower, I came out to find Akmal had already placed a set of clothing on the restroom sink for me. This is why I'll never find another man like him. He knows just what to do to make me feel better.

It seems he's a fan of my tank tops and panties after all because that's all he left behind. There was no way in hell he was going to leave my side tonight, not after what I've been through.

I come out of the restroom to find Akmal changing the sheets on the bed. I join in and we both perform the simple task in silence. But this isn't like that last time, there isn't the same tension but more of a feeling of relief.

We both climb into bed once we're done and come together like we're two magnets that have found each other again. I lay my head on his naked chest as his arm wraps around me tightly, pulling me against his side. I've missed this.

I must have been exhausted from all the crying jags I've had because the next thing I know my eyes are closing and all I hear is the sounds of his heartbeats beneath me.

Something wakes me up. I'm not sure what it is. Is it the light peeking in through the curtains? Something heavy is on top of me and my body comes to life. It's like it knows just how to respond.

Warm hands are running across my exposed belly. It feels good and it makes me hum in appreciation. A body is being pressed up against my side and I can feel he's happy to see me. I don't know if Akmal is asleep and dreaming but I'm afraid to break the spell. I kind of feel like we're still on fragile glass around each other despite having made up from our fight. Was it a fight? I don't even know. I'm just glad it's over now.

I've missed him so much.

I'm still drowsy and languidly enjoying any of the touches he gives me when I feel his body cover mine a little more. I like this, this is nice. I feel like a cat that wants to force their body against someone for more touches.

When his hand pulls my tank top down my legs start to scissor. Oh my. I think Akmal is being naughty and I'm too afraid to push anything in case he decides it's too much and makes us stop.

His hand starts to slowly caress the side of my exposed boob and it makes me melt. It feels so good. I feel like I haven't had sex in a million years and everything is overly sensitive now. Is this the stopped-up horny-chemical's fault? Is it going to make all his touches extra explosive?

When he climbs on top of me fully, I open my eyes in surprise only to see his head go down and take my nipple in his mouth. Holy shit. It's so warm.

I moan when he gives me a particularly hard suck and my hands automatically thread in his hair to keep him there in case he plans to stop before I'm ready. His other hand is already pulling down my other strap, exposing my breasts completely and the cool air sends goosebumps on my skin, making my nipples hard.

I force his hand to my other breast and make him squeeze it hard. Fuck, the things this man does to me and we haven't even had sex yet.

Akmal seems to be on some sort of roll this morning because after a nip, he removes his mouth with a pop and trails his tongue across my chest to the other nipple. Holy hell on a stick. This mother fucking tease is going to make me internally combust right here between the sheets. Speaking of sheets, it's getting too hot in here. My legs widen to bring him closer to me and my hand tries to push away the sheet covering us, resulting in me getting side tracked when my fingers skim over his ass that's currently flexing against me.

"Shit, bite me Akmal." And he does. Damn, this boy can take direction. Where have you been all my life?

His cock is still covered by his boxers but he's pushing against me like it's going to catch on fire anyway. The fabric brings a whole other level of friction against my lady bits as my hips start to thrust against his. His mouth doesn't let up, and soon I feel like my nipples are getting chapped from how much he's sucking, licking, biting and playing with them. The tinge of pain with the pleasure he's giving me is taking me to another level because I feel like I'm getting close to exploding.

I've been letting him lead, afraid to scare him off but I'm too lost in the moment. Both my hands travel down the dip of his back and grab his ass, forcing him to thrust against me harder as I thrust against him.

It hits me like a freight train, making my body shudder and my head push back against the pillow in ecstasy.

"Oh my god." It comes out as whisper and plea all at once. He's got the magic touch. I've never been this easy before.

My hips are still thrusting against him, riding the waves when I feel his cock getting even harder as he continues to rub against me. His mouth pops off my nipple and he buries his face in between my breasts right as he lets out a sexy groan. The warmth that spreads between our clothes tells me he found his release as well.

Cradling him to me, I don't want this moment to end. My hand slowly pets his back up and down as we descend from our mutual high.

What a way to start the day.

Chapter Fifteen

VERO

"What the hell? Why didn't you call me Vero? I could have been there with you!"

"I know, it's just. I was processing, okay. Plus, everything is okay now." Akmal leans over to kiss me on the shoulder from behind and my heart melts into a puddle of goo. He's been more touchy since our little mishap and morning make up session.

I'm finding I really like this side of him.

"Well, as long as you're okay...are you? You know I'm always here for you girl."

"I know, it's just - it was something we both needed to handle. But thank you, Atsuko. I know you're always here for me. That's why I love you." With the word still floating around, I turn my head to watch Akmal open the fridge, shirtless, and look for breakfast. He really is quite a specimen. His smooth tan skin does things to me, reminding me what it felt like this morning when he covered my body with his.

I barely register what Atsuko is talking about when I catch his eye as he straightens back up. We're always like this, searching for each other even when we're in the same room. He gives me a tender expression before he smiles at me and I mouth 'I love you' to him.

His smile gets even wider as he takes steps towards me and pushes the phone out of my hand to give me a scorching kiss on the lips.

"Vero! Vero! Are you listening to me? This bitch right here." Atsuko's voice sounds tiny and far away on the phone's speaker while Akmal continues to move his soft lips against me, dominating my mouth with his wicked tongue, until I'm breathless. He gives me a peck at the end and whispers 'I love you' against my lips before going back to make his breakfast with the items he took out.

Fanning myself a bit, I take a deep breath before bringing the phone back to my ear. "What? What did I miss? And fuck you too bitch, I heard that."

Atsuko is laughing her ass off because she's been the same since meeting Mat. All lovey dovey and shit around me. Well, now I have my own man to be lovey dovey around. The thought makes me want to giggle like a damn school girl even though I'm way past the age.

"Alright you lovebirds. I forgive you. Are you ready for tomorrow? I cannot believe Akmal's family is deciding to make it a double wedding. I mean, it takes a lot of pressure off my back but it's kind of weird, you know?"

"Is it? From what it looks like to me, Mat is like a son to them. I'd be surprised if they didn't offer to make it a double."

"You're right. But still weird. I'm just happy to be able to spend the day with you. Our special day, together. Who would have thought?"

"I know exactly what you mean."

"Alright, this is our last day being single. I say we go shopping and get some hot and sexy lingerie to blow the boys' minds. Maybe throw in a garter belt and stockings while we're at it. You know, make them work for it."

I laugh at that. "That sounds like a wonderful plan. When do you want to leave?"

"I'll be ready in thirty minutes. Meet you at your place?"

"Sounds good. We'll let the boys get their bromance on while we're out shopping."

"Haha, perfect. See you then."

"Bye, Atsuko." Ending the call, I scan the room looking for Akmal. He's walking around the living room looking for something.

"What are you looking for?"

"I don't remember where I put my phone."

"Did you leave it somewhere?" His eyes have a faraway look and suddenly he snaps his fingers.

"Yeah, I did. Are you going somewhere with Atsuko?"

"Yup. Girl stuff. Shopping."

"Okay, well have fun."

"You and Mat should hang out, it might take a while."

"Oh, alright. But I don't have my phone. Can you call him for me?"

"Oh right." Calling Atsuko back, I tell her what's going on and hand the phone to Akmal as Mat comes on the line.

"Yeah, I probably left it at my parents' house. Can you swing by and pick it up for me? Sweet. I guess we're hanging out since the girl's got the day planned. Sounds good. See you soon." He hands me the phone and gives me a peck on the lips while I turn to go towards the bathroom to get ready.

The slap on the ass makes me squeal and turn to find Akmal giving me a boyish grin. *Just you wait, baby boy. I'm going to blow your mind tomorrow.*

"Oh my god, the boys are going to die when they see these."

"That's the plan, Atsuko. At least you can jump on your man whenever you want. I've been dying a little each day with how much we keep trying to hold ourselves back. I cannot wait for tomorrow."

Slipping in the key to unlock the door, we come in to find the boys on the floor in front of their laptops with headsets on.

"Shit, watch out behind you."

"Damn, he almost got me. Thanks bro."

Atsuko and I look at each other with a smile. They can be so cute sometimes.

"Boys, we're home!" Akmal is the first to look our way. How he can hear me with that headset on, I have no idea. But the moment he sees me is the moment he takes it off and disengages himself from whatever he was doing. My heart swells at the full attention he always gives me. It makes me preen like a little bird.

Mat watches as Akmal leaves and sees Atsuko waiting. He does the same and comes to her side.

"What did you get?" Mat and his naughty hands are already trying to peek in Atsuko's bag when she slaps his hand away.

"No peeking! Come on, let's go home so these two can get ready for the big day tomorrow. We have to get ready too."

Mat throws Atsuko a sheepish smile and turns towards Akmal to do his bromance hug for a goodbye.

"I'll see you two tomorrow! Rest up!"

Atsuko looks at Mat over her shoulder and giggles as they leave. I have a feeling they won't be getting that much rest whatsoever.

Once Akmal closes the front door, I walk to our bedroom to put away my shopping bag. Yup, *our room* because he can't kick me out now. I'm too addicted and too clingy. One room away is just too damn far. Plus we'll be married tomorrow anyway.

Akmal is following me around trying to get a peek in the bag when I turn to shove his shoulder and laugh. I swear, these guys can be so naughty.

"Hang out with me?"

"Where else am I going to be? I'm at home with my man. You're not escaping my company that easily." Akmal hugs me from behind and nuzzles my neck. He's so damn sweet.

"I like it when you call me your man."

"Yeah?"

"But I think I'd love it even more when you get to call me your husband." He nips my neck and slaps my ass before walking out to the living room. My god. Who is this man?

"Oh and Vero?"

Once the shopping bag is hidden away deep inside his closet, behind some other things, I answer. "Yeah?"

“Make sure you pack a bag.”

“Why? What for?”

“I just have a feeling. Trust me.” Huh, okay then.

Chapter Sixteen

VERO

What the hell is going on? There are so many moving parts, I'm lost in the sauce, caught in the tornado of Akmal's family and relatives. Akmal told me to send Atsuko the message last night that Saturday, today, will be an early day. We were both so excited we woke up before our alarms anyway. We got here basically at the buttcrack of dawn.

The moment I stepped into his parents house was the moment I realized that a Malaysian wedding is much much different from what I'm used to seeing. Clothes of various colors everywhere and a whirlwind of women all over the place getting things ready. I swear I hear someone mention something about thrones. The house has been converted to a place of ceremony.

The girls are all over Atsuko and I, hands every which way and the next thing you know, we're both dressed in layers and layers of fabric that covers us from head to toe, a soft and flowy hijab accompanied by a small crown on our heads. *Wow.* I kind of feel like a princess from far away lands. I'm not even sure about the actual color of the outfit but there is a mix of soft peach and pinks on me. The embroidery I do see, adds another layer of elegance that makes my heart skip a beat.

This is really happening.

I turn to look at Atsuko and she is in something of a berry red color. It looks amazing against her skin. Atsuko and I were able to do our own wedding makeup and the outfits just took it to another level. I'm impressed with what Akmal's aunts were able to make in such a short period of time.

"Sakinah! Take the girls to do berinai. Your cousin Aryani is already set up."

Atsuko and I look at each other. What in the world is berinai?

"Come on, let's go before my mother remembers something else to put you through. The quicker we get through it, the quicker we get to the actual wedding ceremony." Sakinah is ushering us with quick steps despite her five-foot-three frame.

"Sakinah, what is berinai? Should we be scared?"

She laughs as we continue to weave through all the people here. She brings us to a table with a very friendly Malay woman sitting there ready for us. She has this fat looking pen in her hand. At least, I think it's a pen.

"Berinai is henna. Your continued beautification for your wedding day. You'll love it." Oh, henna. Wow, okay, I'm down with that.

Atsuko goes first and I'm mesmerized by the talent this girl has with her henna pen. Beautiful black swirls and decorations of floral arrangements adorn Atsuko's hands and wrist by the time she's done. Her fingertips are coated with solid black, giving it a slightly gothic feel. It is so beyond beautiful and elegant that my heart wants to burst for her. I'm so happy we were able to do this together.

When it's my turn, I notice the girl change out her pen.

"Why do I need a different pen?"

"Oh, because red will be more beautiful on you and go better with your dress." *Oh.*

The feel of the pen on me and the way her wrist movements flow is mesmerizing. She has a talent that makes it look effortless, and floral designs start to grow along the back of my hand and wrist almost as if by magic. When she starts to color my fingertips in solid red, my heart begins to beat a little harder thinking of what Akmal would say about the way I look in my wedding attire.

Thoughts of Akmal and all the days we've spent together come back to my mind.

"You look beautiful in anything you wear, Vero."

I'm so excited to get this day over with so that I can finally show Akmal how much he means to me. He's seen me at my highest when we first met: my allure, my sensuality, and my confidence. He's seen me at my lowest, when I thought we were going to end. The man I gave my heart to gave me his heart and enough love to put my broken pieces back together.

"I'm stupidly in love with you. I can't even control myself around you. I can't even get a handle on my thoughts. My every waking dream is with you in it, don't ever think otherwise."

How did I get so lucky?

When Akmal's cousin is done, I bring my hands up to admire her handiwork. My gosh. It's the most beautiful thing I've ever seen.

I don't even remember what else happens in the preparation process until the moment my eyes land on Akmal. He's in what I assume to be Malaysian groom attire, a high collared long sleeve top in colors that match my own, with a black hat on top of his head. It's his face that keeps me transfixed as I walk into the room with what looks like a throne waiting for me. *So this is what the girls were talking about.* The flowers and decorations that surround us make everything seem surreal.

But it's the tender expression and one of awe that graces his face that makes me blush, and I can't recall a time that I've been like this. At thirty-three years old, I'm beyond these types of embarrassments, but it seems Akmal has the power to bring them out of me again.

The ceremony goes by in a chaotic blur for me as two weddings are happening at the same time. I can't even hold Akmal's hand for comfort as he sits to my right on the throne. My eyes cast to my BFF's side. Mat's Malaysian attire matches Atsuko's berry red, contrasting his skin tone nicely. They look happy and overly in love. I wonder if Akmal and I look like that?

My heart is still beating erratically from the moment I placed the wedding band on his hand and the moment he places the band on mine. This is it. We're legit. Akmal is finally my husband.

I never realized how tiring sitting around can be until what feels like the hundredth visitor taking pictures with us. Thank goodness for low heels, but my ass is starting to get sore and I'm really starting to get exhausted. I wonder if we get some sort of break time between these visits with the guests? I don't even know ninety percent of the people here. I think I see my family lost in the sea of Asian faces. A few of my relatives too.

Akmal tells me that we *do* indeed get a break and that we're allowed a private bedroom somewhere in the back. Oh, thank heavens. I don't know how long I can sit like a statue up here on this throne. When we reach the back room, I finally let myself relax and let out an exasperated sigh. Damn, who knew Malaysian weddings took this long?

I think Atsuko and Mat were ushered to a different room but I'm glad to get any sort of reprieve from these wedding etiquettes I have to keep up. I'm laying back here on the bed with my eyes closed when I feel warm hands bringing my skirt up.

What is my naughty boy up to now?

"Let me help you relax." *Oh my god.* Is he serious right now? What if someone hears us?

His warm hands push my skirt up over my hips and suddenly a very hot and wet mouth is hovering near my inner thigh. It's such a contrast to the cool air across the rest of my exposed skin. A shiver runs down my spine at the way Akmal has started to come out of his shy shell. *Who is this man right here?*

I'm thinking he's probably just going to tease me when I feel his fingers push my panties aside and a tongue enters my center. *Holy shit.* A whimper escapes me and Akmal nips my inner thigh again to remind me that we're still at the wedding with thousands of people around us outside this little private room. Having to force my lips closed as his mouth tentatively explores my folds and clit makes the moment even more erotic than it already is.

"Vero, you taste so good."

That mouth of his. I can't control my body's reactions when he starts to cover the hood of my clit with his mouth. My hips are already undulating towards his face, silently asking for more as my hands creep to the back of his neck to try and not mess up his hair while still pulling him closer to me. The way his hands start to push my legs apart makes me gasp at his small show of dominance.

"Oh my god."

"Shhh..." That wicked tongue of his is still going to town as he whispers against my pussy to be quiet.

Akmal starts to really pay attention to my responses because soon his mouth and tongue are concentrating on my clit like a champ while his thumb is grazing against my very wet and probably swollen pussy lips. I can feel the tension start to build up, my movements are losing any sort of rhythm it initially had.

Akmal surprises me when he silently crawls up my body to cover my mouth with one of his hands while his other takes over where his mouth left off. The little intermission in his movement didn't stop my internal climb as my body shudders when his thumb does something wicked down there and my cries are muffled behind his hand. Akmal's eyes are sparkling as they watch me enraptured in the climax high, still riding the waves as his thumb continues it's torturous swirl around my sensitive areas. The grin spreading across his face makes me want to fuck his brains out but we still have to wait until the wedding is over.

This bastard is trying to kill me, trying to drown me in a pool of want and need.

And it's working too.

Chapter Seventeen

VERO

I didn't realize there would be a second half to this wedding. Good lord. After some more sitting around and taking pictures with random folks, the wedding party had to get changed again. Now we're in something white with beautiful embroidered embellishments.

As I sit here on the throne with Akmal, I keep catching him peek at me.

After a few pictures and smiles, I turn to my right and mouth 'what?'

Who are these people and why does it seem like we can never get to the end of these damn pictures?

"Nothing." Is that so?

I look to the other throne and can practically see Atsuko internally groaning as well with all these guests.

When Akmal tells me we're allowed another break, I almost run for it but stop myself because I don't want to embarrass him. That would look really bad, right? Girl in white, running for her life away from a wedding crowd.

We're back in the same room and I do let out a groan then. "Akmal, this is crazy. I love you and all, but man, there is *a lot* of Malaysian folks out there. How many more pictures do we need to take?"

He lets out a masculine chuckle and goes to stand by the bed. I need a distraction. I don't want to think about the rest of the night sitting on that damn throne like a princess statue.

Before he can make up his mind, I walk up to Akmal and get on my knees before him. His eyes widen and I can see his hands wanting to push me away but he's not going to, not after I get my mouth on him. My hands go under his top to find...*nice*, an elastic waistband to his pants. In one swoop, I have his pants down to his ankles and am face to face with an already semi-hard cock.

He wanted this too. The sneaky bastard.

Gripping his cock in my hand, I'm entranced by the henna at the back of my hand against the tan skin of his cock. But time is of the essence and I have a mission to make this man fall to his knees.

With a lick up the slit of his opening, I can hear him groan under his breath as his cock starts to become much harder, and much, much bigger. Teasing the head with the tip of my tongue, I flatten it under his shaft right before taking him into my mouth. I love the way he tastes. Like a damn forbidden fruit because we shouldn't be doing this right now but hell if we're going to stop.

Giving him a low hum so as to not expose us, Akmal's dick twitches in my mouth. I guess he likes that. Shit, I like it too. I love the way he responds to my mouth taking him in deeper and deeper.

When my mouth reaches the end of his shaft in a slow glide, I swallow and preen at the fact that there's some lipstick stains against his skin. When I swallow again, Akmal groans a little too loudly. Pulling back, I whisper 'shhhh' to the head of his cock before taking him in again and again.

I can taste the precum on the next glide, letting my tongue play with his slit one more time before going in for the kill. Taking him as deep as I can, my other hand plays with his balls as I make my throat swallow. He starts growing in girth and I think I can feel his hand softly behind my hijab as his hips twitch and his cock spurts jets of cum down my throat, which I eagerly take in. Can't leave any evidence now, can we?

When his dick slows down in his climax, I start bobbing my head again to make sure I clean him up before putting him back in his pants. Nothing can be done about the ring of red lipstick against his skin now. Oh well. Sorry not sorry.

When I stand back up, Akmal grabs me and nuzzles against the layers of fabric at my neck. I love it when he's like this.

"Good lord, I can't wait until this day is over. I can't even touch or kiss you in case your makeup gets messed up and people start to question what's going on." His hands are roaming the back of my neck and my ass, only serving to make me hotter than I already am. These layers of fabrics aren't helping either.

When our break is up, I quickly find Atsuko to see where I can find lipstick to reapply. She gives me the look, telling me she knows exactly what we've been doing and we both giggle together under our breath as we try to fix the issue before anyone else notices.

Once we're back at our thrones, I'm trying hard not to rub my legs together. I'm so worked up. Fanning myself between taking pictures, I look around to see if my family is having a good time. My parents are talking to Akmal's parents and no one's yelling, so that's good. Some of my aunts and uncles are mingling well, lots of smiles.

Scanning the room a few more times, I notice I can't find my damn brother anywhere. Where the hell could he be?

SAKINAH

After the stress of this morning, I'm very glad this wedding is going well. Everyone looks happy, especially my brother. I've never seen him so happy like this. I wonder what my wedding would be like? Would I find a man that looks at me the way Akmal looks at Vero? Like she is his world. Just the thought of all the Malay boys

I've been around has my stomach turning. Ugh. Just no. Sometimes I fear that anyone I might be interested in would be related to me somehow, someway.

The guests are finishing up their meal and so that gives me a break from the rush. Walking outside, I take a deep breath of much needed air, closing my eyes and just letting the cool breeze blow against my skin. It feels wonderful and refreshing after being in that hot kitchen.

"Sakinah."

I startle at the sound of my name in such a deep voice, a voice I've been trying to avoid all day. Turning around, I see Fabian looking at me with something devilish in his eyes. There's no other way to describe it, with the aura he always gives off. He's trouble on two legs, I know it, but it doesn't stop my feminine fantasies from coming to life, though I don't let it show on my face. Guys like him don't need any more of an ego boost, he has plenty of it with the way he swaggers.

"Fabian."

"That's it? Just Fabian? No - where have you been? Hey, sorry I didn't get to come by and say hello?" I give him a small smile. He's fishing. No, I'm not sorry I didn't go by to look for him. I wouldn't want anything to happen that might embarrass my family or my brother on his big day.

He chuckles at my silence. "Like that huh? I thought we were past this 'strangers' stage Sakinah."

"So you say. What are you doing out here? Wouldn't your family be looking for you? You should be mingling with the crowd."

"I am mingling. With the only girl I've been looking for all day." My heart skips a beat. Is he serious? He's been looking for *me* all day? I can't let him see me weak. Guys like him would pounce on that and use it to their advantage. My mouth still tingles at the thought of his kiss - my first kiss.

"Well you've found me. Did you need something?"

"Well, for one, since we're basically family now, how about we exchange numbers in case of emergencies." Emergencies, my ass. The only emergency I see happening is this guy getting himself into some sort of trouble. Do I really want to be involved in that?

Watching the way his biceps flex against his button-down long sleeve top that looks too small for his large frame as he reaches the back of his pants to grab his phone, my body's saying yes, yes I would. But my mind is telling me to stay away from Fabian Hernandez and his steel grey eyes with lips that are much too soft to be true.

I don't have my phone with me, so I just put my number into his when he passes it to me. Once I'm done, I leave him there, standing without another word.

"Okay, be like that. What can I do to make you give me a genuine smile my way?" He's sending me a cocky grin that would make any woman's panty melt. He really shouldn't be that good looking.

"How many times has that line worked on the other girls?" Fabian puts his hand over his heart like I've wounded him and I laugh at how ridiculous he looks. This shouldn't make me like him more than I already do.

"Come on, don't be like that Sakinah."

"Like what, Fabian? Like a girl who wants to make sure you have the best of intentions? Don't be perasan la."

"I do have the best of intentions. And what does that mean?"

"Don't flatter yourself." He chuckles and it's the most masculine sound.

Looking him up and down, the man is walking sin. And now he's a liar.

"No, you don't."

"Alright, alright." His masculine chuckle sends shivers down my body. It's a good thing I have so many layers on, he probably didn't notice. "I may not be the perfect guy but I can be good. How about friends then, hmm? Surely we can be friends?"

Is he really asking me this? Especially after stealing that kiss from me in my own home. Now I'm kind of upset with how easily he gave up on chasing me. Am I just a passing game for him? Well, you know what? Screw him. I knew I shouldn't leave my guard down around a bad boy like Fabian.

"Yeah, we can be friends." No, I really don't want to be friends.

He smiles even wider, causing cute wrinkles to show up at the corner of his eyes, transforming his face into something that would stop any woman's heart. I can't do this. Turning abruptly without a goodbye, I leave him there as I walk back into the mingling wedding crowd.

Some of my brother's university friends are standing around and chatting. Walking by I make sure to give them my greetings and show a friendly face to the crowd.

"Sakinah, is that you? Wow, you've changed since the last time I saw you. You've grown into a beautiful woman. Is that why Akmal doesn't talk much about his -" I'm blushing at the compliment and turned confused at why his sentence got cut off. His eyes are looking over my shoulder and so I do the same.

Fabian is standing behind me, grey eyes blazing down at Bisaam. What is wrong with him? I give him a frown but he's still not looking at me.

I can hear Bisaam clearing his throat, so I turn and give him and the guys around him what I hope is an apologetic expression.

Slapping Fabian's chest with the back of my hand, I clear my throat as well to get his attention. Once his eyes are on me, I mumble, "Can I speak with you outside?"

His eyes give Bisaam one more glare before he follows me back out the way we came. Rude, much? How embarrassing.

When the door closes, I twirl around and give it to him. "What is wrong with you?"

"What do you mean what is wrong with me?"

"You're supposed to be acting like a friend, isn't that what we agreed upon?" We're alone out here, letting me raise my voice a little more than I would if we were inside.

"I am. I just wasn't liking the way that guy was staring at *my friend.*"

"Who does that? Look, if you can't control this -" My hands are waving in front of him to indicate all of him. "-friendship, then maybe we shouldn't be friends."

"Don't be like that Sakinah."

"Like what?"

"Nobody should be looking at you like that."

"Why not? What if I like the way they look at me? What if I'm looking for a husband huh? Why are you blocking my chances at finding someone?"

Fabian growls and it does something to me. I feel a little excited, my face flaming a little but I'm not going to show him that I'm affected. Not with the way he's acting like I'm not worth the chase and yet I can't get compliments either? He can't have it both ways.

"Don't say that shit to me Sakinah." What is wrong with this guy?

"I don't even know what you're talking about. I'm twenty-five and my mother has already been hounding me about finding someone so I can make babies for her before I'm past my prime. Might as well get started. Plenty of men around at this wedding. It's the perfect opportunity." Am I fishing and being petty? Maybe.

We've been turned away from each other slightly during this entire ridiculous conversation. What is up his ass? He's the one that basically told me he wasn't interested.

Chancing a glance at him, I see Fabian turn his blazing molten gaze at me right before he pushes me up against the wall, grabs my face in his hands and kisses me. Oh, this kiss is nothing like the one he stole the other day, not at all. This one is dominant, and quite frankly a little scary. His lips and mouth are coaxing something from me and I don't know how to respond. This is not like the movies where you think you want it. This is so much more *intense.* I open my mouth to try and tell him to stop when his tongue takes the opportunity to invade. The moment our tongues touch is the moment his hard grip on my face softens and one of his hands travels down to rest at my neck, encasing it in its warmth. I shouldn't like how this feels. I shouldn't like how his tongue expertly glides against mine, making me curious where this can lead.

I should be scared. I shouldn't let him put me in this position. *I'm being too easy.* He just told me he wanted to be friends. What the hell? Is this how he treats all his female friends? The thought kind of pisses me off and sobers me enough to allow me to shove at his shoulders and give him a slap on the face before turning to go back inside.

Chapter Eighteen

VERO

I've been told that Akmal's family has paid for a hotel stay for both wedding couples. How very kind of them. Knowing that fact, now I'm even more antsy to get away from the formalities of this wedding. How long does a Malay wedding go for? Please tell me it's only one day and not multiple.

"Akmal, I'm getting kind of tired."

Akmal gives me a sympathetic look and calls his mother over. He speaks something in Malay and she is nodding her head with a smile towards me. "That is fine, you guys go find your bapa and he will drive you to your hotel room huh. The guests can leave whenever they want, do not worry. We will handle everything."

Oh thank heavens.

Soon both wedding couples are packed into Akmal's father's vehicle with our bags. I guess Atsuko and I will be in the same hotel.

He drops us off with a smile and says something to Akmal about making lots of babies before leaving. *Geez*. At least you never have to wonder what they're really thinking.

I give Atsuko a hug as we go our separate ways down the hallway. I can already hear Atsuko squealing on the way to her room and it makes me smile. Akmal sticks the key card in the door and once it opens, we're greeted by conditioned air and silence. Perfect.

My husband brings our bags in and is already falling back on the bed with a sigh of relief. I take it upon myself to grab my necessary items before heading to the restroom to change. I'm excited, the day is finally here. All this pent up energy is giving me a second wind as I strip quickly and grab the stuff I bought with Atsuko.

The lace is so beautiful and soft. I really hope he doesn't rip it.

Once my stockings are firmly attached to my garter belt, I take a step back and look at myself in the mirror. Not too shabby. I like it. It looks hot. He better not fucking rip this shit. Well, unless he makes it worth it.

Turning the doorknob, I let the restroom door open by itself to its full extent as I stand there canting my hips to the side for the full sexy effect. With the hijab off my head, I was able to mess my hair a bit to add to the sexed look factor.

Go broke or go home, right?

Akmal is lying on his back in his boxers, relaxing with his arms behind his head, flexing his biceps in the most delicious of ways. When the restroom door hits the wall with a soft thud, Akmal lifts himself partly on his elbows to look at me.

The way his eyes widen and scan me from head to toe is priceless. A look I'll never forget. *All for you, baby.*

"Holy shit..." It's spoken under his breath but I can hear it from where I'm standing and it makes me feel a sense of pride.

Sashaying towards him, Akmal slowly gets up to a sitting position to see me better. I'm loving the way his eyes keep going to my breasts and they start to feel heavy under the lace. The memories of his mouth over my nipples, sucking and biting, makes my pussy tingle and I haven't even reached him yet.

"Did you buy that for me?"

"Yes." Oh what is this coy smile on his face?

"You look fucking beautiful." Hearing those words on his lips never gets old. I've been told I'm attractive before, but the way Akmal says it is so much different.

Giving him a seductive smile, I start crawling over his lap as he starts to lie back down with his hands behind his head in what looks like a relaxed posture. Is he not as pent up as I am right now? Making sure I keep my ass in the air, I slowly rub my lace covered breasts over his chest and trace his jaw with my fingers. He really is too sexy.

"Well, hello...wife."

"Hello, husband." Crawling a little more, I start with a chaste kiss until we're building up the heat that's been stoked since the pre-wedding days. Akmal and I have been at each other for so long, pushing and pulling, that I was starting to think my pussy would explode from the moment he enters me.

Our kisses are soft and coaxing, but soon become hot and heavy in a matter of minutes. What I thought was me seducing him has now become him dominating my mouth with his. *How the hell did he get so good at this?* My body has become lax on top of his, dropping my weight down entirely, as not only his mouth, but also his hands coax me where he needs me to go. I'm internally purring like a damn kitten with how he's petting me and making me pant for more.

I'm drowning in his kiss when suddenly I feel my boobs fall out of my bra, making me gasp. I didn't even feel him unhook the clasp. Without taking his lips off mine, Akmal removes my straps and tosses the bra to the side. His hands return and are all over my breasts, pinching and pulling at my nipples with just the right amount of pressure to make me feel it in my pussy.

Gasping into his mouth once more, Akmal surprises me by flipping me over and settling himself between my legs. *Holy hell, who is this man?* He's grinding into me slowly with his hard cock and my breath stutters with how hot we both feel down there. The friction between his boxers and my lace panties aren't helping one bit.

"Are you a dirty girl, Vero?" *Oh my god.* Akmal loves to kiss and sneak in statements like that between kisses so I can't think straight or respond. When his lips and teeth start to travel across my jaw and down my neck, my body feels strung tight from the day's anticipation. His warm hands are caressing my lace garter belt and panties all the way down to my stocking-clad legs.

Raising both my legs up, I wrap them around him and start to slide them against his hips. His mouth continues to leave a wet trail as he goes lower and lower. Taking my right nipple into his mouth, his hand starts to play with my left. I've never met a man who sucks like he does. It's hard, it's erotic, it's the thin line between pain and pleasure. His teeth will nip, his lips will suck and his tongue will soothe. It's torturous and I can't get enough of it.

When Akmal's mouth travels to my other nipple, my fingers thread through his hair and cradle him to me. I love how he worships my body, like I'm a damn five course meal to be savored. We've probably learned the art of slow seduction and foreplay from all the edging we've been doing since our engagement.

My eyes are closed and taking in all the sensations when I feel him going lower and pulling down the top of my garter belt.

"Fuck, I knew it." His whisper is so soft, I barely caught it. Opening my eyes, I look down at him as the tip of his tongue plays with my belly button ring. I can feel my skin getting goosebumps from the cooling wetness on my breasts, adding another layer of sensation.

Akmal gets up on his knees and I watch as he stares at my center, legs spread eagle for him. He leans in with an arm on the bed and grabs the front of my panties, dragging it back and forth against my swollen pussy lips, making me squirm.

"You have the prettiest pussy I've ever seen." I'm probably the only pussy he's ever seen but it doesn't prevent me from feeling my heart swell with his praise.

"Are you wet for me, Vero?"

"Yes."

"I bet you are. Just look at you. Fuck, I can't believe this is all for me." He's pulling the panties back and forth even harder and it's starting to hit my clit just the right way, making me whimper.

"Open your legs up for me." Shit, how far does he want them to go?

I must not be opening far enough because he rips the lace panties off me, making me yelp from the pain of the snap, and pushes my legs apart with his strong hands right before he dips his head down to lick my pussy. *Dios Mio.*

"I love the way you taste. Always so wet for me." When he hums into my pussy, the vibrations start a climb I'm desperate to chase. How does his tongue do these wicked things to me? Is it because he's become more comfortable with my body and expressing himself? Fuck, that thought turns me on even more.

His fingers are rubbing over my lower lips as his mouth starts to play my clit the same way he sucked and played with my nipples. Shit, he is aggressive and I love it.

"I want your fingers in me."

"Yeah?"

"Yes, please." He groans and sucks my clit even harder after my plea.

"I love the way you say please."

"Please Akmal!"

"Are you a good girl? You've been so bad this whole time." Oh dear lord.

"I've been good."

One finger slowly enters me and I feel like I'm dying, on the precipice of almost there and not quite.

"That feels so good."

"Shit, I can feel you squeezing me. I can't wait anymore." I'm in such a haze of lust that I growl in frustration when he removes his finger and mouth to step out of his boxers. He chuckles as he climbs back on top of me and kisses me again, the taste of me still lingering on his lips. I'm so damn horny, my hands grab his ass and pull him to me.

His shaft starts to slide against my wetness as he drags it up and down a few times.

I'm groaning in frustration again as I grab his cock, the feel of him like velvet steel, and line it up against my pussy. I need him now!

"Fuck." He impales me on his next stroke and just glides in from how wet I am.

"Oh my fucking god." He leans in and tucks his head into the crook of my neck, bringing his hips back to push in again. Fuck! Either he's bigger than I thought or I've gotten tight from the lack of sex.

Kissing the side of his neck, I whisper into his ear. "You feel so good. I'm so damn full."

"Shit, Vero, I'm not even in all the way yet." Holy mother of ...

Bringing his hips back he shoves in one final time and buries himself to the hilt, making me feel even more deliciously full to the brim. It's as if something becomes unleashed because Akmal starts pounding me into the bed with stroke after stroke.

His grunts next to my ear make my pussy clench around him, only serving to make him add groans.

"You feel so fucking good, Vero. Hell, I didn't know it would feel like this." I can't concentrate on how his words make me feel when I'm climbing again, chasing an orgasm with the way his hair is rubbing against my clit with every forceful stroke.

I'm so close, so close. His thrusts are becoming faster and faster as we both chase that proverbial cliff to fall over.

"You feel so good." The moment the words leave my mouth is the moment Akmal bites down on my shoulder, starts to grow in size and thrusts deeply into me a few more times before he cums. The way his hips grind deeper into me like he's afraid of slipping out ignites the fire that sends me over the edge with him. Holy shit.

His continued grinds against my oversensitized clit keeps my climax on a high and sends me through aftershocks that rock my fucking world. This has never happened before. I'm almost glad we've been messing around for the past week since his stamina is better than what one would consider for a guy who's never done it before.

He plants his lips on mine and starts to make love to me with his mouth as he continues to ride the fall of his release, going from deep thrusts to slow and leisurely ones. This man continues to amaze me. How did I get so lucky? This is a first - I feel like my heart is going to burst. My eyes are getting warmer as if they're about to cry.

"I love you, Akmal."

"I love you too." We're kissing like we have all the time in the world when he abruptly pulls his face back, confusing me by his change in demeanor.

"Shit, I didn't pull out. Did you want me to finish in you?" This cute baby right here is looking so sheepish it makes me want to laugh. But I hold it in because I don't want him to feel worse.

Pulling him back towards me for another kiss, I whisper against his lips, "I'm on the pill. I want to feel my husband cum in me."

He groans and whispers back against my lips, "You're such a fucking dirty girl, Vero."

When his cock slips out, I can feel his cum leaking out of me, making me squirm again. Watching the way Akmal stares at how his release is coming out of my pussy is starting to rev me up again. He looks so damn possessive at this moment. When his fingers trail up the mess and shoves back in me, I whimper from the fact that I'm still oversensitized by the recent climax he's given me.

"So fucking dirty..." Biting my lip, I'm excited to see what kind of lover Akmal turns out to be. It's been nothing but surprises so far and my pussy is more than willing to go another round.

Chapter Nineteen

AKMAL

That was the best experience of my life. I never thought it would be that intense. I was trying to tease her, to hold out, to make it good for her. I know she has more experience than me and I wanted to be able to bring something to the table. With the way she grabbed my cock and shoved it into her, I'd say it went as planned.

Holy hell, the feel of her vagina gripping me is like nothing I've ever known. I think I'm addicted. Watching as my cum leaks out of her pussy does something to me, makes me feel something I haven't felt before. Pride and possessiveness. Fuck, that pussy is finally mine and look how she glistens.

I want to touch her again, but I also don't want to make her uncomfortable. How much is too much? All those days I've caught her in the shower are coming back to me and I like where my mind is going.

Grabbing her hand to pull her off the bed in an embrace, I grab her face and kiss her again. This never gets old. I love the way her soft lips feel against mine.

"Let's go shower."

"Oh, let's ... together?" Grabbing her hand and pulling her to the restroom, she doesn't ask any more questions. Turning on the shower head to let it warm up, I start pulling at her lacey outfit, impatiently trying to get her naked as fast as I can. She chuckles at me as she starts the slowest undressing known to mankind. Looking over the beautiful creature that is mine, I notice that she has a tattoo on her right shoulder and another one on her left hip. It's cute and very Vero. A little surprise wrapped up in beautiful clothing.

I need to make sure no one ever sees what she has underneath. The thought of other men looking over her smooth skin makes me want to punch something. Damn, I'm starting to understand Mat's obsession with going to the gym. If this keeps continuing, I'm going to need to do something to exorcise these emotions.

When Vero turns around to bend over and take off her stockings, my dick jumps up at the offering. Damn, her ass is the nicest I've ever seen. Her pussy lips are still glistening with the evidence of what happened earlier, reminding me that I need to get her wet under the spray and wash her body.

She's doing this slow tease again, pretending to take her time to remove the stockings entirely. Grabbing her by the hips I bump my hard cock against her ass to hurry her up. She squeals and I give her a good slap, making her straighten her back. Good. Ushering her into the shower, I slide the door close, step in with my back to the spray and grab her face to kiss her again. She can be such a brat. I know she does this on purpose, killing me slowly.

Maybe she wants to be punished. Maybe that's what I've been missing by not reading her clues. Does Vero want me to put her in her place?

Stepping back, I let the water slide down her chest. Grabbing the soap from behind me, I start to lather my hands and slowly rub it all over her body. She's so fucking beautiful, especially the way she looks at me when I take care of her. I love this look on her. I need to make sure to always keep it there. Her breath hitches when I make sure to go over her breasts a few times, pulling and tugging on her nipples. The water drips down and washes away the suds, making my eyes trail down with it. My fingers trail after them, entranced by the way her abs flex and her breath picks up.

Vero leans into me, pressing her breasts against my chest, and slides her hands up my shoulders right before I take her in another kiss. It's slow, it's steady, unrushed. All the pent up frustration has been worked out of us and now it's just time to explore each other.

My cock is rising fully to attention at the way our bodies glide against each other. I need to feel her again. Pushing her around, I bend her forward, letting her hands hold her against the shower wall as I slide my cock between her legs. It's a different kind of wetness, I understand the difference now and the difference makes me impatient to feel how well I can slip into her pussy. Vero arches her back, silently asking for it. I'm learning to read her now, the way her body responds, the way she moves when she's pushing for more.

Grabbing her hips, I stare at my dick as I slowly thrust into her. Fuck, she's beautiful like this. The way her ass moves when I pound into her. Something inside of me makes me feel a need to mark her. To know that I'll be the only one to see what I leave on her skin. Yes, that's exactly what I'll do.

Slapping her ass, I start pounding into her, leaning forward on top of her to lick the water off her back. She's moaning and it spurs me on, makes me even harder for her. Grabbing her hair, I tilt her head back and kiss her again as I continue to thrust hard and fast, her wetness giving no resistance to the brutal pace I'm setting.

Squeezing her breasts, I lick the shell of her ear and ask her, "Do you like feeling my cock in you, Vero?"

"Yes."

"Fuck, this pussy belongs to me now."

"Oh my god."

"You're not sleeping tonight, not until I've had enough."

Straightening myself back up, I lift one leg onto the ledge of the shower and start drilling into her. I can feel the tension creeping up my abs and my balls start to tighten as I chase my climax. Vero is moaning louder, the sound of the water coming out of the spray no longer being able to drown out her cries. My grip gets tighter as I fall over that cliff I'm getting addicted to, Vero's pussy taking everything I have to give her.

As my thrusts start to slow, my cock slides out and I turn her around for another languid kiss, washing her under the cold water. She squirms when my fingers slide into her, trying to clean her as best as I can while we're both still in here.

I'm getting sidetracked by the way she pushes her breasts against me again every time my fingers graze her clit. Unable to help myself, I forget to wash her altogether and start to swirl my thumb between her legs as my mouth sucks on the crook of her neck.

It doesn't take long for Vero to reach her peak, her body shivering and her legs giving way. My arms go around her as I cradle her in an embrace, my mouth making love to hers again under the water spray.

SLEEPING NEXT TO MY WIFE IS THE SAME BUT NOT. There isn't that push and pull anymore. Now, it's just my wife's beautiful warm body, waiting to be taken.

She squirms in her sleep and I pull her in closer, smelling her, memorizing the moment. *My wife, she's finally mine.* We don't have to be anywhere and it's nice having that burden taken away for the day. This photography job came at just the right time as it allows me to make my own hours to be with her.

I kiss the back of her shoulder, dragging my lips along her smooth skin. I didn't let her get dressed last night before we ended up falling asleep making love with our mouths. Her ass presses against my crotch the more I tease her skin and the morning erection I have is starting to twitch in anticipation of what we might get away with.

Slowly gliding my cock between her legs, I can feel her growing wetness. Her legs are scissoring and her thighs are squeezing my cock, making it grow harder with her movements. We're both lying on our sides, snuggled under the sheets but it's starting to get hot, the air getting thick with what's working up between our legs. My hand trails down her shoulder and arms to toss the sheet off us, letting the cool air of the room try to control the blazing inferno happening right now.

"...Akmal..." I love the way her voice is so breathy and low in the morning.

"Shh...go back to sleep." Lifting her leg, I slide my cock inside. The pressure and heat around my shaft is still something that shocks me everytime. But like a damn addict, I can't help but keep coming back for more. Vero has to have the tightest pussy with the way she takes all of me in her.

With a groan, Vero pushes her ass back, letting me trail my hands down her spine, pushing her back forward so that I can see that delectable ass of hers as I thrust inside. Shit, she's so perfect for me.

It's starting to feel too fucking good to be in this position. Pulling out of her, she cries in protest as I get my knees on the bed and lift her ass to follow. Vero doesn't resist and moans when I take both of my hands and spread her ass for my viewing pleasure. She's so damn wet for me all the time, glistening and waiting for me. The cool air of the room is sending goosebumps along her skin and my hands rub it down with its warmth.

But we can't let her get too relaxed. Vero likes to be a little brat sometimes, just like right now with the way she keeps backing her ass up against me, hoping that I'll impale her again. I shouldn't make this easy for her though. She's been playing my body for a damn week with how she's been teasing me, torturing me slowly.

Squeezing her ass and spreading her cheeks again, I tell her, "Vero, turn around."

She follows commands so well, it makes my dick leak. I bet she loves this.

"Open your mouth." There she goes, following without any sort of protest. In fact, her mouth swallows my dick down so far, I almost cum right there. *Shit, she's too good at this.* The taste of herself on her lips doesn't bother her one bit. She continues with her ministrations and swallows every now and again when my dick is all the way inside to the back of her throat. *Fuck.*

"I love your mouth sucking me. I knew you were dirty, Vero." My hands creep to the back of her head tentatively. I'm not sure how much I can push. In my fantasies, I've been doing such dirty and wrong things to her.

She hums and brings her eyes up to mine. I love this look on her with my dick in her mouth. She worships it like she'll die if she can't do it. It makes my heart swell with love at the moment. My fucking wife, goddam.

It starts to feel really damn good and I don't realize I'm gripping her hair and thrusting into her face but Vero continues to hum in pleasure, sending vibrations down my shaft. I can see the saliva dripping down her chin and I know I want to finish in her mouth. That first night with Vero that changed everything will always play in the forefront of my fantasies.

"Are you going to be a good girl for me, Vero?" She doesn't nod her head but speaks with her eyes instead as her mouth continues to work up and down my shaft, sucking harder at the end in tune with my thrusts.

Damn, just look at her. "That's a good girl, fuck yes, just like that."

Who knew praising her would make her double her efforts. If she keeps this up, I won't last much longer. I groan out loud at one particular swallow when she has my dick down her throat despite her nose being up against my body.

"Shit, if you keep doing that, I'm going to cum in your mouth." She sucks me in deep again, almost making my eyes roll back. "You want that don't you? You want me to cum in your mouth."

When I feel my abs tensing, I try to hold back my climax and start to really shove it down her throat hard. Vero has stopped her momentum and let me take the lead. My grip tightens behind her head, trying to hold onto the smooth strands that are trying to run through my fingers. I can hear myself grunting as my hips hit her lips over and over again. She gags a few times and for some reason that shit just spurs me on even more. *Damn, I'm enjoying that way too much.*

When she whimpers it makes me feel powerful. *I love the way I affect her*. Her hands have come up to hold onto my thighs but she never pushes me back, no. In fact, she's encouraging me to fuck her face harder and faster. Who am I to deny her what she's asking for? In and out, in and out. On a particularly hard thrust she gags again but never pushes me away. Her eyes tear up and it turns me on only because I know she wants this as much as I do.

"Shit, baby. That's a good girl. Take my cock in your throat, just like that." She whimpers again and I can feel my balls tighten. I shove my cock down her throat and hold her face there as I feel my dick pulse and cum, watching how she continues to swallow everything I have to give her. *Fuck.*

When my balls start to empty, I rock slowly into her mouth, letting her savor anything I have left to give. *I love having a wife that swallows*. My hand loosens it's hold on her hair and I pet her face as she continues to lick the head of my cock.

"You're so beautiful, and you're so good to me." She removes her mouth from my cock, pushes it up with her hand and licks the underside like it's fucking ice cream.

"You make me so horny, Akmal." She whispers against my dick, while she continues to lick it clean. My hand continues to pet her and caress her face as she looks up at me from where she kneels.

"Yeah?"

"Yes. I'm so horny. Please." Look at how she begs. I think I can get used to this. She begs so prettily.

"Come here." The excitement in her eyes is hard to miss as I lie on my back, coaxing her to sit on my face. She doesn't disappoint, rubbing her pussy right at my mouth wantonly, not waiting for any more commands.

I love the way she tastes. But I love the way she squirms over me even more, knowing I hold her pleasure in my hands. Sucking and licking her clit with my tongue, I slide two fingers into her, listening to her gasp above me. Thrusting in and out, Vero starts to move her hips with the motion, seeking more friction. Adding another finger, Vero starts to moan. I can feel her pussy occasionally clamping down on me, hoping for something more, something bigger. All these years pent up must have given me more stamina because my dick is rising to her pussy's call.

Her lower lips are swollen and wet. Removing my fingers, they start to trace a pattern on her pussy opening as my mouth plays with her clit and nips at her hood. I can feel her tense up now and again but I'm feeling a little selfish.

With one last hard suck on her nub, I flip her onto her back and shove my hard cock back into her, pounding her like we're both rushing to win the race. She cries and moans but I want to get deeper. I need to feel more of her around me. Grabbing her thighs, I put both of her legs on my shoulders and lean into the bed and her body to pound into her harder. *That's it, yes. This is the angle.* It feels so much fucking better.

When her nails dig into the side of my arms, my hips hit her harder and suddenly Vero is constricting my dick like it's trying to choke it out. The people in the next room can probably hear her cries but I can't stop. Not now. I'm so close.

Vero releases her death grip and covers her face with her forearms. A few more thrusts and I can feel my sack wanting to empty again. One, two, grind. I growl as I climax inside of her pussy that's still pulsating around me. Damn, all those years of virginity are worth it to meet a woman like her.

Her legs slip off my shoulder, letting me press my body against hers as I share a slow and sensual kiss with my wife.

Chapter Twenty

VERO

I can't take my eyes off him. It's like the floodgates have been opened and I'm not sure I know who this is, this version of Akmal. He's morphed into something that makes me want to beg, makes me perk up and see if he demands something of me with a look or a smile.

We've been at it like rabbits all night and all day, for two damn days. I was almost feeling dehydrated a few times with how many times he's been keeping me up. Thank goodness for room service because we did not leave the room at all during this honeymoon period.

But today is checkout day. I'm ready to go back home. I think Atsuko texted me sometime a while back that they already left for home, only choosing to stay one night and day at the hotel Akmal's parents got for us. They're used to fucking on every surface though. For me and Akmal, we had some build up we needed to get out.

"You ready?" The grin he throws my way makes me rub my legs together a little bit before getting up from sitting on the bed. The drive home was peaceful and quiet. Akmal, being the cheesy guy he is, insisted he perform a proper bridal carry over the threshold of our home. He can be so sweet.

Once we settle back in and unpack our bags, Akmal brings up a conversation I didn't see coming.

"Vero, are you planning to keep working at the bar? I mean, as a bartender at the restaurant."

"Yeah, I guess. I never really had any plans beyond it. Why?" Akmal is quiet for a few moments and I'm unsure of how to feel.

"You know, my photography business is starting to get bigger. You wouldn't have to work at the bar if you don't want to." I never said I didn't want to. But now that he's brought it up, the question is in my mind. Do I want to stay there? When I was single, it was easy to find quickies. But since Akmal came into my life, I found that I couldn't care less about that fact.

Maybe it is something to consider. But what would I do outside of bartending? I was a few credits shy of finishing my associates degree. I still didn't have a particular direction or major I wanted to work towards.

"I don't know, babe. I never really thought about anything outside of it, I guess. What would I do?"

Something crosses his features, like he's been itching to say something this whole time. "You can always come work with me."

I laugh at that. What would I do? I don't know the first thing about taking pictures. Sure, I can pose and look sexy in front of the camera, but that's about it in that regard.

"How is that going to work? I don't know how to work the camera, not like you. And plus, you have Mat as a partner for that."

"Yeah, but if we pick up more gigs, we won't have much time behind the scenes to work the website, answer emails and respond. By the time we finish photoshoots, we both have to come back and still do edits." I guess he makes a point. I start to think about it, really think about it.

His hands cup my face and bring me to his lips for a chaste kiss, stalling whatever thought that was starting to shape in my mind. "Vero, be with me. It makes my damn chest burn knowing that I can't be there with you at work. Knowing that other men are looking at what's mine, planning ways to take you from me."

Well, when he puts it that way...who knew Akmal would be so possessive? I love it.

"What if I want to keep working as a bartender serving other men?" I'm being a brat. I know. Akmal's eyes start to burn into mine.

He grabs my ass and picks me up, making my legs wind around him. Sitting down on the bed, I thought I was going to be in for some sexy times, when his strong arms maneuvers me so that my body is hanging over his thighs instead.

Smack! Smack!

I squeal like a little girl. Where the hell did that come from? My ass is throbbing with phantom pain still left behind until Akmal's warm hand starts to rub at my ass, soothing it away.

"What was that for?" Sometimes, I just can't control my mouth.

Smack! Smack! Smack!

My god. "You know exactly what it's for." He doesn't rub my pain away this time and I pout, but it doesn't change his mind one bit.

He rolls me onto the bed and gets up, continuing on like nothing happened. The audacity -

"You're coming to work with me, Vero. That way I can keep that sassy mouth of yours out of trouble. I don't need you riling up other guys while I'm not around to punch them in the face for even looking at you." My heart wants to burst at that and I'm silently giggling into my forearms as I lie here on my stomach on the bed.

I think I like riling up my husband.

Jumping out of bed, I jog to catch up with him. I find him sitting on the couch with a computer on his lap. Just like that, I feel like being a brat again. He just ups and leaves me in the bedroom and doesn't even give a rat's ass, does he?

My plan was to distract him but instead once I'm close enough, Akmal pushes his laptop to his side. He then pulls me onto his lap sideways, giving me a soft kiss on the neck. "Look at what I have pulled up. This is what I want you to do for me. Then I won't have to think about what your ass is doing in whatever outfit you're wearing and how other guys around you are affected." I'm laughing my ass off. *Who is this man?* I love how much he's coming out of his shell.

Grabbing the laptop with one hand, Akmal brings it to my lap. I love the way his forearm flexes and I start to wiggle my ass a little on top of him. Akmal bites my shoulder, making me gasp.

"Stay still, I'm trying to show you something." He's getting bossier and bossier, isn't he? Makes me just want to go against him to see what my punishment will be.

"I'm going to need you to keep track of the inquiries that come in, organize them and let me know before you schedule them. Can you do that for me?" He's kissing my neck while asking me these things. How the hell am I supposed to think straight?

"Yeah, I think I can do that."

"I might need you to get in front of the camera for me when I get new lenses in, to make sure they're working properly." I can feel his warm breath and wet tongue licking at my skin now. It makes me start to breathe harder. Akmal, the damn tease.

"Okay."

"Maybe I'll need you naked, to make sure the lighting is right against your skin." Oh.

"Is that so?"

He nips my neck, right before saying, "But if anyone looks at you I'll kill 'em. So it's going to have to be a bedroom shoot only."

I think my panties are soaked. Akmal scoots me off his lap and gives me a kiss on the forehead. What just happened?

"I'll give you some time to get used to how the website works. I'm going to call up Mat to check up on him after all the festivities. You should have Atsuko come hang out to keep you company." He's really serious about this. He wants me to quit bartending so I can work with him.

"Okay." My mind is still trying to wrap itself around the concept of being a family-owned business as I start to ring Atsuko.

"Hello?"

"Atsuko! Are you free today to come over?"

"Of course! I took some time off because of the wedding. When do you need me over?"

"Right now would be cool. Akmal is calling -"

"- Mat. So that's who he's talking to. Yeah, of course. Give me thirty minutes and I'll be there. Do you need me to bring anything? I'm surprised you guys came up for air after the honeymoon." We both laugh and it lifts my spirits about this change in my life that's about to happen.

"I'll see you in thirty."

"See you then."

Akmal is already rubbing my shoulders as I end the call.

"I'm going to be out and about with Mat today, maybe see if we can find some more clientele. Will you be okay here?" Placing my hand on top of one of his, I give him a gentle squeeze.

"Yeah, Atsuko's coming over."

"Good. You two stay out of trouble. Especially you." What the hell is that supposed to mean? I never find out because Akmal kisses me senseless, making the computer slip off my lap and onto the couch right before he leaves.

Chapter Twenty-One

VERO

"That's so kind of him! He just wants you with him all the time, afraid some guy is going to sweep you off your feet when he's not looking. How cute is that?" I'm hanging out with Atsuko in one of Akmal's t-shirts since we're not going anywhere.

"I mean, when you put it that way, yeah it's cute as hell." We both laugh because I've been talking to Atsuko about how Akmal is coming out of his shell. She loves it and I do too. It's a nice surprise despite the fact that I was initially attracted to shy and nerdy Akmal. Dominant and commanding Akmal makes me squirm.

"So you're going to be their metaphorical office girl?"

"Yeah, it seems so. What do you think? Should I still try to fit in time bartending?"

"Why? Mat has been talking to me about them getting more inquiries and how he really has a good feeling about the photography business booming. Plus, we know some people from the circles we've hung around to help them build up more clientele." She's right. Together, we would be a powerhouse with a lot of potential growth.

"How about you Atsuko? Are you jumping on this photography bandwagon or are you sticking with the makeup counter?"

"I never really thought about it. I mean, the makeup industry brings in a lot of money and I don't work there full time."

"Aren't you worried about the female clientele that might be a little too interested in your man?" Atsuko's eyes blazed at that mention, her lip curling into a small snarl. I knew she didn't think about that fact. After all the woman drama they've been through. Who am I kidding? I'm being selfish because I want my BFF to work with me.

"Are you still holding onto that makeup job, Atsuko?"

"Ugh, I'm going to have to think about it. The thought of someone touching my man makes me want to kill a ho." Oh, I know. Atsuko and I grew up in a rougher neighborhood. We're not afraid to get our hands dirty.

"Don't think about it too long chica, I can't beat them all off for you. I'm supposed to be working." I can see the cogwheels spinning in her head. Good, she really doesn't need another obstacle in her relationship.

"What are your plans with modeling, Vero? Are we still doing it? I remember us talking about trying to get contracts. Life has really thrown us a curveball, huh?" Yeah, it really has. The days of daydreaming together about getting contracts and living the high life has now been put on the backburner. Or rather, more important things have come up like finding our significant others and getting married. I don't regret it one bit, because YOLO.

"Alright chica, let's get our head into the game. I mean, *I need* to get my head into the game. I do secretly love the fact that Akmal is possessive of me so I need to really make this work so he doesn't fire my ass." Atsuko is laughing her ass off, the bitch. But I love her.

"So, what are you supposed to do? Just emails?"

"I don't know, Akmal just kind of threw the computer at me and told me to get familiar with the website."

"He must have a lot of trust and faith in your abilities then. Alright, let's look at it together."

We both straighten our postures on the couch and scoot close together as we scour the photography website. To be honest, Akmal and Mat have got some mad skills. These photos are amazing. But the amount of unread messages dates back to a couple of weeks ago.

I called Akmal once to ask if he would allow me to start scheduling and he proceeded to link his calendar to mine. How he did that, I have no clue. But he's a brainiac so I just go with it. Both Atsuko and I start to answer emails and write down possible scheduling on paper before committing it on the digital calendar.

As a team, I think we did pretty well. It wasn't as stressful as I thought it would be. Mentioning that fact to Atsuko, she seems to agree. Good. Maybe she'll consider teaming up with me. We're basically family after all.

The boys came back in the late afternoon, Atsuko and Mat not staying long after that. Atsuko had helped me get an early dinner ready while she was here and now I'm sitting on the couch sideways with my legs on Akmal's thighs as we watch some mindless television.

"So, we should be getting more emails for inquiries soon. We ran into some students at the university."

Laying my head back on the arm of the couch, my toes start gliding under the bottom of his shorts. "Okay, I'll keep an eye out. You have a photoshoot this coming Thursday."

Taking a swig of his beer, Akmal nods his head to let me know he heard me. "Yea, Miss Williams. She had scheduled it a few weeks ago. I think she mentioned needing updated headshots and body shots for her modeling portfolio." Putting the beer on the coffee table, Akmal starts to massage my feet. He's so good to me. "She mentioned that the beautiful girls on my page were what convinced her."

I've seen his page, the only girls he has on there are me and Atsuko. That's flattering.

"So I'm free advertisement hey?"

"Just showing everyone what they can't have." Akmal has gone from massaging my feet to kissing up my calf. I'm getting goosebumps with the way his eyes are smoldering into mine, there's an intensity in them that makes me fill with a sense of anticipation. How did I go from miss confidence around Akmal to this, to always anxiously awaiting to see how he plays my body? I continue to watch him as he slowly moves like a predator on the prowl.

He pushes my shirt up over my breasts and exposes me to his gaze. His groan slash growl makes me clench between my legs. "Vero, you're not wearing any shorts or panties."

"No, I'm not. Why should I?" Akmal, groans again at my response.

"The mouth on you, woman." I was going to give him another retort when he steals my breath away with his tongue diving into my pussy. This is where my confidence has gone, into the man before me devouring me like I'm his dessert he's been waiting for all day.

Opening my legs wider, Akmal situates his shoulders until the back of my thighs are on them. Relaxing my head back against the arm of the couch once more, I take in all of the sensations he's bringing out of me. When his tongue dips in and flicks up at the tip, it makes my body arch with his ministrations. His thumb is staying busy, rubbing my clit in circles and it's driving me mad. It feels like I'm riding a high wave with no reprieve of fluctuation and no end in sight at the same time.

I can feel my abs tensing but not enough to get there. He's killing me. I start to whimper as my body automatically starts to inch away from him but Akmal has other plans. His hands grab my ass and pull me back to his face as his mouth attacks my clit with a different kind of fervor. Sucking and nipping, the tip of his tongue teases the underside of my swollen hood and I can feel myself climbing.

The hands on my ass are gripping hard and the occasional sting of the nails biting into my flesh makes me rock my hips against his face this time instead of away. What is he doing to me?

Right when I'm about to orgasm, Akmal pulls his face away and gives me one slow and savory lick up my pussy and to my clit. He raises his head with a devilish smile while I'm about to throttle him in my mind.

It must show on my face because he chuckles as he climbs over me and flips me over like I weigh nothing. I don't know when he pulled his shorts down but when he covers my body with his warmth, I can feel his cock tapping up against my wet pussy like a tease. It's desperate to get in and I'm desperate for it to be in me. Reaching down to do just that -

Thwack!

My ass still stings as Akmal grabs his cock and starts slapping it even more against my core. A few more dick slaps and Akmal is gliding his cock along the wetness, coating his shaft. Everytime the head of his cock bumps against my clit, I moan to ask him for more. Seems he likes to be in control and any attempts I make to get to my finish gets me punishment. Torturous, slow-teasing punishment.

I love it and hate it.

Preparing to be teased to no end, it catches me by surprise when Akmal sticks the tip inside of me before going back to gliding his cock against my pussy lips again. Dammit!

A small growl must have escaped my lips because his hand starts to pinch and tug at my nipples as he bites down on my shoulder.

It feels so damn good, and I'm already so worked up that I might just cum from this. The sensations are starting to climb again when Akmal leans away, bringing cool air across my back, grabs my hips and shoves his dick right to the hilt. He sets a brutal pace and I fall off the hill I was climbing into an almost painful climax that doesn't slow him down one bit. Shit shit shit. This is too much. Too much.

"Shit, I can't take it. It's too much."

"You're going to take it." One of his legs goes to the floor for more leverage and I almost feel like he's pounding my face into the arm of the couch every time his hips hit my ass. I fucking love this side of him.

"You feel so fucking good Vero, taking it like a good girl." Oh my god. My climax was just starting to plateau when his words stir something in me.

"You like this don't you? Bent over and taking my dick like this."

"Yes." I can barely get the words out with the way my face is getting smushed into the cushions of the couch arm.

"Damn, I can feel your pussy gripping me. I'm going to cum. Shit."

"Yes, cum in me. I want it, Akmal. You make me feel so good." He really fucking does. Has sex ever felt like this? No one has ever read my body and my mind like he does with the stuff that comes out of his mouth for my ears alone.

A few more thrusts and Akmal is groaning as he leans back over me, nuzzling against the crook of my neck. I can feel his hot breaths tickling my skin, making my hair move when he whispers, "That's a good girl. Make sure you keep that mouth of yours out of trouble."

"...what if I like trouble?"

He bites my ear as his hips continue a slow rock until his cock slides out. The feeling of our combined wetness dripping down my thighs makes me want to go another round. Maybe I'll be a brat again, just so he can punish me.

"Don't be a brat, Vero. I know you're thinking about it right now. Just be a good girl."

Damn, he's good.

Chapter Twenty-Two

VERO

The Thursday appointment wanted to do a photoshoot at a parking garage another town over. Apparently this one is hardly used, giving it an abandoned vibe. The model is a gorgeous African American woman with legs for days. Her beautiful curly hair only adds to the whole package.

Akmal is too busy adjusting the settings on his lense to notice the girl looking at him with hunger in her eyes. I'm a little ticked but I get it. He's hot. He's even hotter when he doesn't notice you. There's just something about that. I know, because that's how he got me.

Once he's ready, the model starts posing over the outer edge railing, simulating overlooking the city. Her profile is gorgeous and she knows it. There's a confidence in her swagger, the way her hips move, the way her eyes look like they're enticing the man behind the camera - my man. I'm rationalizing in my mind that this is what models do after all, I've been in front of the camera, I've done it myself.

But that was when I was single. Apparently, married Vero is a possessive and jealous bitch. The more the model sticks out her chest and her ass, the more I want to punch her in the face.

Akmal isn't helping anything by telling her she's doing a good job, asking her to pose certain ways to help with lighting against her skin tone in this dark garage.

I can't help but feel like all of his praises belong to me. I'm also bristling at the fact that the model, Miss Williams, is obviously preening every time she hears a praise out of his mouth. *He is mine.*

A few hundred shots and clicks later or whatever it is, Akmal gives his little talk about how he will get back to her as soon as possible after edits. The same talk he gave Atsuko after our photoshoot at the car show. He's showing her some of the raw images through the viewscreen at the back of his DSLR camera and I can feel irrational fury growing within me with how close Miss Williams is standing next to him.

Breathing in and out slowly, I try to calm my thoughts. This is his job, this is what he does. Get it together.

Time fucking slows as I watch Miss Williams put her hand gracefully on Akmal's shoulder to lean in a little closer to 'look at the raw images'. Her eyes are really giving him side glances and I swear I can see her nostrils flare from taking him in.

I'm seeing red. The Puerto Rican and Hernandez side of me tells me to take this bitch out. The wife side of me is telling me to calm the fuck down because this is his business that might get affected by my behavior.

I'm warring within myself but I'm still shooting daggers at this ho in front of me right now. She doesn't see me of course because she's secretly sniffing my man.

My hands are about to involuntarily rip her hair off when Akmal gives her a polite smile and steps away, messing with the buttons near the viewfinder. My man is always so clueless when it comes to flirting, thank God for small blessings.

When her eyes find mine, she gives me a polite smile and proceeds to pretend to adjust her tiny outfit. *Bitch, don't act like you don't know what you just did.* Or maybe she doesn't know. Maybe she thinks Akmal is single. It's not like she was looking at his finger.

Walking towards Akmal, I lean my body right up against his, sliding one of my hands on his opposite shoulder, my finger starts playing with his ear. Leaning in to look at the viewfinder too, I kiss his neck.

"Those look great, baby. Good work."

"Yeah, I think we'll be able to turn over edits quickly with this set." My oblivious husband.

Oh, but Miss Williams isn't oblivious. Her eyes are watching our interaction carefully. I know this look. This is the look of a woman still waiting to see if she can squeeze herself in between despite the fact that I just laid claim to my man.

I got my eye on you chica.

Narrowing my gaze at her, we both communicate mentally. Whether she takes my warning to heart or not, we have yet to see. It's a good thing that I'm pretty confident Akmal is going to make her edits look amazing so there wouldn't be a reason for her to come back for another photoshoot.

Akmal being the kind and clueless man he is, tells her he will take a few more shots just to make sure he can find the best photos to help build her portfolio. This time around, she's sticking her ass out even more provocatively, sending bedroom gazes his way and through the camera lense. I'm getting pissed again but she hasn't backed off one bit. No, in fact, she's issuing me a damn challenge.

The hood bitch in me is already clawing her eyes out. I'm trying damn hard to be the bigger person here. Staring at the back of Akmal's head, he's still clueless as ever. I know I shouldn't be pissed at him, but the more he angles his camera and the more he leans in for a 'better shot', I'm about to blow a gasket.

The rest of the session ends in a fog because my mind is just constantly repeating the crap I saw that woman pull off in front of my husband. Being a photographer, I can't ask him to look away. It's his damn job. *Fuck, get it together Vero!*

But he's my fucking man and I worked hard to get him and keep him. I'm like a boiling volcano with how much I'm trying to keep this shit inside. A girl can only do so much as tears start leaking out on the drive home.

Holding back any sniffles, I turn my face to look out the window and just breathe slowly. I shouldn't be this mad, I shouldn't.

Pulling up at our apartment, Akmal only notices something wrong when he opens the passenger door for me. Squatting down, Akmal cradles my face in his hands and has the most concerned look on his.

"What's wrong, Vero? Why are you crying?" Because women are trying to take him away from me and he's so damn nice and innocent that he wouldn't even know what's happening until it's too late. Then where does that leave me?

I don't know what's come over me but I storm out of the car and into our apartment, straight into the damn kitchen to find something to stuff my face with so I can concentrate on something else.

The sound of the door closing and locking tells me Akmal is trying to walk on eggshells around me. Good! He should with how unstable I'm feeling right now. Dammit! We didn't buy any more ice cream.

Slamming the freezer shut, I remove my shoes and layers of clothes until I'm just in my bra and undies before crawling into bed and letting my frustrations get smothered by his pillow. The warmth of his arms around me only serves to make me feel worse, I don't know why.

"Vero, talk to me."

"I don mmf wanno." The pillow is muffling my face, but I don't care.

"What happened? We were having a good day today. It made me happy that you were with me while I worked." I know. I know it does. I could see it in his eyes when he would sometimes steal glances at me. I'm being stupid. But that bitch was throwing it in my face and I couldn't do a damn thing about it.

Akmal, the perfect husband he is, rubs my back to try to soothe whatever is happening in my mind right now. Chaos. It's utter chaos in here. How do I explain that to him? He'll probably think I'm nuts.

He's calling my name I think, but I'm lost in thoughts of all the other women out there who schedule to get photo's done by my sexy as sin husband. What if I'm not there everytime to make sure to stake my claim? What if girls start to do more than just a touch? Is he even going to know how to fight off their advances? He doesn't even know how to read advances.

"Tell me what you need."

Lifting my head off his pillow I mumble, "Ice cream."

"Got it. I'll be right back." And off he goes. This is exactly why women are all over him. Why can't he just be perfect for me at home and a jerk everywhere else? I take that back. Girls like that shit too.

I managed to calm myself down by the time Akmal comes back with ice cream, mostly because of the ice cream. Akmal sits on the couch next to me with his arm slung behind me. I'm feeling good, until he starts talking about her.

"That was a good set, she looked really good with the shadow and the way the sunlight filtered through. I think this is going to be an easy set to edit." She looked good. No... he said she looked *really* good. The fuck?

My spoon is stopped midway to my mouth and I shove it back into the container. Placing it slowly onto the coffee table before us, Akmal still looks like he's off in photographer land while he thinks about this woman's curves.

I mean, I could castrate him but that wouldn't benefit me when I get horny.

"Akmal..."

He's lost staring into nothingness, having to shake his head a little to give me his attention.

"Yes?"

"Please don't tell me how good another woman looks."

"What? I didn't say that. What are you talking about?"

"You just told me she did."

"I was talking about how the photo session went well with the lighting and such."

"You didn't notice her touching you?"

"When did she do that? I don't remember this." Figures.

"She was touching your damn shoulder when you guys were looking at the viewfinder on the camera."

"Vero, I don't even remember any of that. I mean, I remember showing her the raw images so she can get a feel for what to expect. It's how I do things so the client feels confident in the final product. Why are you getting on me like this?"

"What do you mean why am I getting on you like this? I'm your fucking wife and I don't like other women touching what's mine." When did I become this person? And I can't seem to stop once it starts.

Akmal is sitting up straight by now, his hands in a placating gesture and even that makes me pissed. I'm not a rabid dog, even if I feel like tearing that woman's throat out.

"I didn't let her touch me, I'm telling you Vero. I don't remember any of what you're saying. Just calm down for a sec -" Oh hell no. Calm down? CALM DOWN?

"What the hell do I need to calm down for Akmal? Are you saying I'm making shit up right now? Because I saw what I saw and a woman knows when another is sniffing around her territory. I don't like that shit. I'm from the hood. We handle that shit quick, fast and in a hurry before it can grow into anything else. I was being the bigger person by holding myself back while you worked." Shit, am I breathing hard? My head feels tight, like more word vomit is about to come out of me without my permission.

"Vero, Vero... stop. Just relax, nothing happened between me and her."

"Fucking hell! I know nothing happened between you and her, I was there remember? It's just you're so...you're so..." I growl in frustration at my lack of ability to form a cohesive sentence despite there being a million words in my mind right now.

Getting up, I throw the carton of ice cream in the trash since there were only two or three bites left anyway. I'm sure I'm stomping like a petulant child as I go to the bedroom and start getting dressed to go out.

I must have left Akmal in a stupor from my womanly hissy fit because he's still there staring at the wall trying to process everything. The moment my keys jingle from the hook in the kitchen is the moment Akmal jumps up and turns around to look at me.

"Where are you going?"

"I need to calm the fuck down like you told me to Akmal. Isn't that what you said? I need to *calm down*? Well let me go and do just that." I'm riding the high of my anger. Nothing makes sense and everything makes sense. My mouth and body is telling me what to do but my mind is telling me that I'm overreacting because he's right, nothing happened.

I just need to get away from Akmal's cute face and his stupid hot body that's walking towards me, making me feel weak. Rushing out, I slam the door in his face and run to my car that hasn't been used in the past few weeks. I'm backing out and driving like a bat out of hades and I don't know why I feel so rushed. Not until I pull up to mi Mamá's house.

Chapter Twenty-Three

VERO

"Oye. ¿Que pasa? ¿Por que tu está aqui? ¿Está todo bien?" My mom is always able to read my moods like the back of her hand. No, things are not alright. I should feel bad for worrying her like this, but my mind is all over the place.

"I'm fine, Mamá. I just had a fight with mi esposo." She's giving me a look that says 'so what?'. Now I really feel stupid about how I acted. I've seen my parents argue all the time but they're still just as tight together as I remember too. Nothing can break them apart. How do I become like that? Am I being petty?

Once I'm in the door, I can hear my dad's voice talking to Fabian about something. Fabian is always over here despite having an apartment somewhere. What a waste of money. But with his seasonal construction job and carpentry on the side, he's got money to spare.

"Alejandro, tu hija is home!" I can hear the sound of heavy footsteps leaving the carpeted area and coming onto the hard floor of the kitchen.

My dad has always been my main man growing up. He used to feel like such a big presence to me. Once I became an adult, I realized despite him just being a five-foot-seven average Puerto Rican male, he's still my safe space when I feel needy.

Like right now.

"Vero! That was a beautiful wedding." He stops when he sees me and then takes the last few steps to give me a hug. "What is wrong, Vero? Dónde está tu esposo?"

I left him at home because I can't trust myself to not explode and mess things up. I don't tell my dad that though, he doesn't need to worry about my marital issues.

"Vero, what happened? Who's ass do I need to kick?" Fabian, despite being a jerk sometimes, is also my other safe space.

"It's nothing guys. I just... I just need to clear my head a bit."

"Clear your head? What did Akmal do? Why are you guys fighting already?" Fabian can be astute when he wants to be.

"Come on, let's go watch some TV." My dad is still holding me as he escorts me to our outdated floral couch. My mom follows behind. I don't know where Fabian is.

Lying down on my side I put my head on my Papá's lap and just let my mind drift as we watch one of my Mamá's telenovelas.

FABIAN

Whatever this fucker did to my sister, I'm going to find out. But the only number I have is Sakinah's. As my fingers scroll through my contacts, I quit lying to myself. It's just an excuse, I wanted to find a reason to call her anyway. Well, good, now I have one.

It takes almost five rings before she decides to pick up. This girl, she likes to leave me hanging. She's probably doing this on purpose because she knows it's me. I can't help but like the annoyance she brings out of me.

"Hello?" The breathy sound of her voice makes my cock twitch. I miss the taste of her lips.

"Sakinah."

"What do you want, Fabian?" Sassy little shit, isn't she? I wonder if she throws this sass to her parents or is it just me? I'm probably just special. At least that means she thinks about me. Hopefully in the ways I've been thinking about her. Does she get wet? Is she waiting for me to come back around? She seems a little too old to still be living with her parents. But look at my ass, I'm here all the time.

"Hurry up, I got things I need to do." Fucking hell. I bet that pretty little mouth of hers would look good around my -

Get your head in the game Fabian.

"Vero came home upset and shit. What did your brother do?" I can't let her see how much she affects me anyway, that'll give her the upper hand. There's a pause before she responds. If I was standing next to her, I'd make her talk in the best of ways.

"I don't know. He's not here with me, he's probably still at his apartment. Why don't you call him?" The mouth on this girl.

"Because I only have your number, or did you forget when you slapped me and walked away?" I can hear her intake of air on the other side. Yeah, I didn't forget that and I know she hasn't either. I also didn't forget the fact that she didn't complain about it when I brought it up. She probably thinks about it just as much as I do.

"I'll call him and let him know where she is. Bye Fabian." Fuck. Just like that she hangs up on me. What is it with this woman? Good girl, my ass...

Walking back into the house through the backdoor, I find my sister laying solemnly on my dad's lap. What happened?

"Vero." She jumps at my voice, not even seeing me standing here for at least a minute or two.

"What happened? Tell me."

"It's stupid."

"Tell me anyway."

I watch as she takes a big sigh and sits up with my parents on either side of her for emotional support.

"He wants me to work for him."

"Okay..."

"...and we had this photoshoot with this girl who was beautiful. She kept flirting with him. I couldn't stand the way she was trying to homewreck me. She had that look, you know? It's the same way Juana looks when you know she's about to cause trouble."

Well shit, Juana is our local desperate housewife. I mean, she's single but she wants to be someone's housewife, even if that means it's with your husband.

I can see why Vero would be cautious about this.

"But why are you here then? Shouldn't you be over there making sure that shit doesn't happen?"

"I was! I mean, I was trying to tell him that but I'm no good with words when I'm pissed. It all comes out jumbled and then he tells me to calm the fuck down and -" I can already hear my dad choking and my mother cursing under her breath.

Every man should know this rule. Never - and I mean never - tell a woman to calm down. Especially a Puerto Rican Hernandez woman.

Chapter Twenty-Four

AKMAL

What the hell is going on? I must be losing my mind because I swear I don't know what happened or why it ended up this way. I've been driving around town for a good thirty minutes when my sister Sakinah calls me.

"Hello?"

"Akmal, Vero is at her parents house."

"How did you know she even left? Can hah? Are you sure?" That's a bit strange. Did Vero call her? Why would she do that? Wouldn't she call Atsuko first?

"Fabian told me. He was worried about her. Fix this, I don't want to lose my sister-in-law already. I like her." Shit, I'm not about to lose her. I love that woman too damn much to let her get away from me.

"Alright, thanks for letting me know. I'm going to fix this. Thanks Sakinah."

"You're welcome." She hangs up and I look at my mirrors before swinging the car around in a u-turn.

I should have checked her parents' house instead of driving around. Well, we found her now. It takes me a good thirty minutes more from where I started to reach Vero's old neighborhood. I can see her car parked out in front and Fabian's car in the driveway.

Pulling up the vehicle right behind Fabian's, I throw it in park and quickly run up to the front door. I didn't realize I was banging the screen door so hard until it started rattling. I'm kind of pissed and kind of worried about my wife. Worried she's really upset and pissed because I didn't do anything wrong.

Fabian opens the door with a glare. Reminding myself of my last thought, I cross my arms and stand up straighter.

"I'm here for my wife." We're staring each other down for a few moments before he stretches out his hand for a handshake. I don't know what is going on but if it gets me closer to my woman, I'll do it.

"I'm glad you are, I'm tired of her mopey ass attitude." Did she really take it that badly? Walking into the front door, I turn to ask Fabian what I'll be walking into when he says under his breath, "A word of advice my man, never tell a Hernandez woman to calm down, bro."

Shit. Duly noted. Nodding my head I start walking past the kitchen to the living room. Vero has her back turned to me as she stands there staring at the small box television sitting on a stand in front of the couch.

"Vero, it's time to come back home." At the sound of my voice, Vero whips around and my heart tightens a little at her look. She looks like she's fighting something on the inside and I'm not sure if I should be worried.

Not letting her get any time to think she can run away from me again, I grab her arm and pull her in for an embrace. Kissing the top of her head, I just hold her until I can feel her body relax.

"Thank you Mr. and Mrs. Hernandez for taking care of my wife. We'll see you guys later."

I can see Fabian nod his head at my actions over his father's head and I turn towards the front door with Vero still in my arms.

"Are you alright?"

"Yeah."

"Alright, let's go home."

"Okay." She sounds so small and vulnerable that it makes me want to punch something for her.

The drive home is quiet and Vero doesn't look my way, choosing instead to stare out the side window of the car.

The moment we step inside our home, I lock the door and turn to settle whatever it is that's going on. I don't even get a chance to gather my thoughts when Vero lays it on me.

"Why did you have to tell me how beautiful she is, huh? And then when I try to tell you as your wife that she was being a snake, you have to take her side...over me? How do you think that makes me feel?"

What the hell? I'm getting kind of pissed again because we're going around in circles here, wasting time fighting over nothing. She turns away from me but at least she's staying inside this time.

"How the hell am I supposed to keep working with you when I know for a fact all these beautiful model women are going to be all over you during these shoots? Makes me want to fucking pull my hair out when you're all nice and shit to these girls. Makes me want to pull my hair out because I know you have to be for your job."

She's rambling, continuing to walk away from me and frankly, I'm tired of this attitude she's giving me when - again - I didn't do a damn thing wrong. When we pass the bedroom doorway, I grab her arm and spin her towards me, slamming my mouth on hers just to make her shut up for a moment.

She's being difficult as she starts punching my chest like I'm not her damn husband demanding my right. Winding my arms around her tightly, I squeeze her until her breasts are rubbing against my chest, preventing her arms from making any more impact.

Coaxing her lips to open up for me, she continues to refuse in her stubbornness until I move my lips to her chin and nip at her skin. She tastes good, even in her fury. She tastes like my wife who's being a damn brat about this whole thing that has been blown way out of proportion.

Sucking at the skin at her neck, I can hear her start panting, her arms loosening their tension, no longer trying to push me away. Taking this exact window of opportunity, my lips find hers again, my tongue spearing inside to convince her to submit to me.

She fights, of course she does. Because this is Vero, she's always been that spitfire that ignites my hunger even when it was from afar. To know that she's just as possessive over me as I am over her makes me feel good. Damn good. I must be doing something right then.

Our lips and tongues continue to fight it out as I start stepping us closer and closer to the bed. Ripping at her top without stopping our kiss, Vero gasps into my mouth which only makes me more determined to get where we need to be.

The fabric falls to the floor leaving her breasts only restrained in a bra. Too many obstacles. Too many damn obstacles. She does this on purpose, I just know it. Challenges me to see how far I'll go for her.

When I end the kiss, she whimpers in protest until she feels my hand jerk the cup of her bra down and take her nipple into my mouth. The room is getting hotter by the minute as she buckles and falls back onto the bed, me landing right on top of her. She's not getting away that easily, oh no.

"Akmal..."

I bite on her nipple before moving to the other. I'm going to have to make a no bra rule when in the house. I hate this shit. I need to feel more of her. The tension I felt earlier from my initial fight is coming back to me in full force.

Popping my mouth off her other nipple, I start to quickly strip her out of her pants. She pretends she's fighting when in reality she lifts her hips here and there to help me remove them.

Dammit, panties. She needs to be naked and available to me at all times. Tired of fighting scraps of fabric, I lift her leg to slap her ass before turning her over with her legs hanging off the bed. Perfect.

Vero is already glistening as I lick up her pussy. When she starts to shift and wriggle, my hands find her backside a few more times, watching my handprint disappear. Her skin was made for that, made to be punished.

"Vero, get on your knees."

"No, I'm still mad at you." I laugh out loud as I lean over, grab a fistful of hair, pulling her back for another kiss. This woman kills me. When her body starts to soften from our tongues dancing, I pull her off the bed and down on her knees.

Her eyes are blazing as they look up at me while I undo the button and zipper, freeing my hard cock in front of her face.

"You keep looking at me like that wife, I like punishing you." The flames spark into something else and I know she wants this just as bad as I do. Vero loves to be put in her place.

"Be a good girl and open up." And she does, letting me shove my dick right down her throat. She gags and tears up but her hands also come up to start stroking me in tune with her sucks.

"That's it. You're always being a brat because you want this, don't you? You just want to be forced to be a good girl on your knees."

Her eyes sparkle and she starts to bob her head and suck harder. Fuck, I can't last when she's enthusiastic like this.

She moans and the vibrations go up my shaft, making my gut tighten at the sensation.

"Fuck Vero, do you want me to cum down your throat?"

She pops her lips off the tip, licking my slit right before she whispers, "yes."

I want to cum down her throat. But she's been bad and she shouldn't get what she's asking for. That's like rewarding bad behavior.

Pulling my dick out her mouth, I grab her and throw her on the bed face down. Lining up my cock to her entrance, I impale her and start pounding my frustrations out. Leaning over her, my hands find her clit, wet from our friction, and start circling and pinching. Her back bows and I know she's found her chase. My thrusts slow down as my fingers pick up speed and soon enough Vero is screaming my name, the feeling of her pussy convulsing around me making me want to let go too.

But I can't. No, not yet. It's not that easy after what she put me through walking out that door.

I push her onto her stomach, releasing my dick from her pussy and turn her around. She doesn't need any direction when her mouth finds my cock again, one of her hands still playing with herself to prolong whatever it is she's feeling. Do girls cum back to back? From the way Vero's eyes flutter, it must be so. The little cheat, finding her pleasure when she's supposed to be getting punished right now. I give her a soft slap on her face to take her out of the moment and concentrate on the task at hand. My little dirty girl gets back into the moment and starts sucking like her life depends on it. I can feel my balls wanting to tighten but I'm holding back. I want to make her work for it, work for it harder.

My fingers slide under her hair and grip it hard to slow her tempo, my hips thrusting into her face instead. Shit, this shouldn't be so hot. Vero at this point has fully submitted, letting me do whatever I want without complaint. In fact, she's moaning and loving this shit.

I want to cum in her, but not like this.

Pulling her head off my cock, I let it fall back on the bed as I lift her legs up and cross them, making her pussy tighter for me right before I shove it back in. It doesn't take me long in this position, Vero bent almost in half, for me to find my release. And when it arrives, I feel like I'm seeing stars from how long I've been holding myself back, the shock of the orgasm going down my damn spine.

Vero moans even louder as jets of my cum shoot into her. Fuck, it feels good. I continue to thrust into her slowly, making sure to bury myself as deep as I can go. I bet she would look beautiful carrying my child. In fact, I need to fuck her brains out and keep her pregnant so she never leaves me again. The thought makes me pound into her some more before my cock finally shrinks and slips out.

Chapter Twenty-Five

VERO

Akmal didn't let me rest at all for the past week. I don't know what's gotten into him but I secretly love it, even though I tell him he's pissing me off. The expression that darkens his face makes my pussy clench because that's when he gives it to me the hardest, when my mouth gets the best of me.

From the kitchen table, to the floor, to up the wall. Akmal has been insatiable. I'm hanging out with Atsuko today, so Akmal is just going to have to hold himself back before he makes me late. Once I finish up my wiggle dress with some heels, I walk to the kitchen and grab my keys. The jingle makes Akmal come up behind me with a hug, his kisses going down my neck. Shit, I need to leave before I don't want to leave.

"Baby, I gotta go. I don't want to make Atsuko wait by herself by not showing up on time."

"I like it when you call me baby."

"Yeah?"

"Yeah, it makes my cock hard." God dammit Akmal. Turning quickly, I give him a peck on the lips and run out the door before he can pull me back.

I can hear his chuckle right before the door fully closes. Letting out a long breath, I fan myself as I walk to my car. Atsuko wanted to meet up at Sammi's, the sandwich shop we met the boys at on that fateful day. The day I started injecting myself into Akmal's life until there was no one else around him but me.

The drive was short, the cool breeze outside making it fresh when I let the windows down. Christina Aguilera's Nasty Naughty Boy makes me think of Akmal when I know I shouldn't be.

By the time I walk up to the metal table outside, I see Atsuko sitting there with her legs crossed in her pencil skirt and heels. Gorgeous as always my BFF is. Her siren red lipstick stands out against her light complexion. In fact, we must be in tune with each other because I think we're wearing the same lip shade.

"Hey! Vero, you made it."

"Of course, were you waiting here long?"

"Nah, just about five minutes or so. You're good."

"Did you order yet?"

"No, the waitress told me she'd give me time so that she can wait for both of us to order at the same time."

That's exactly what we do when Atsuko starts bringing up the real reason for this meeting.

"I was thinking about what you said, about us working together with the boys' business venture. The other day he went on a photoshoot and was telling me about the model. I almost went to her house and gutted her, I was so mad on the inside. Of course, Mat is oblivious to that shit." She must be reading my damn mind or we have to have been twins in another lifetime.

"Girl, I just went through the same damn thing with Akmal. Had a fight over it too."

"Yeah? How did you handle it? At least you were there! I was at work thinking of all the worst case scenarios."

"Yeah, that would be worse. You need to come work with us. It's the best way to keep an eye out for homewreckers."

"You're right." We've been chatting and eating our sandwiches, just about finishing up when I think I hear my name being called, by a male. It can't be Akmal. He's not that paranoid when I'm out with Atsuko.

Turning around my heart drops to my stomach, making it churn into something nasty feeling.

There standing a few feet away from me is my ex - my high school sweetheart, Roman fucking Guzmán. High school bad boy who played in a rock band. He looks older of course, gained some mass on him and maybe some height. His dark features are still as cocky as I remember too. The waitress comes out to take our empty plates away and she lingers a little longer than she should, probably checking this fucker out. *Yeah, I know, tall, dark and handsome.* But the way he left road marks on my heart makes bile want to rise up my throat.

"Roman."

"Vero!" He's shooting his signature panty melting grin at me and I almost do puke. Is he serious? Is he fucking serious right now? The bastard that played me for a whole damn school year just so he could take my virginity and fucking run?

"You've got the fucking nerve talking to me right now Roman."

"Aww, don't be like that. You know how high school is. We're beyond that now. I saw your face -" As he proceeds to look at my body up and down. And yes, I did grow even more into myself after high school. "- and just wanted to say hello to an old friend."

I turn my face towards Atsuko, who's been quietly shooting serrated knives with her eyes at this fucker, and lift my lip in a snarl. This asshole. Oh yes, I've told her all about this fucker.

We both look at each other for a second and get up, bending over a little to smooth down our outfits. We're both in something skin tight and Roman doesn't limit his perusal to just me. Once a snake, always a snake.

We're just about to walk past him when he has the audacity to grab my arm to stop me.

"Vero, if you ever want to hook up again, I'll make it up to you." I see red.

The punch that lands on his face, knocks him into one of the metal chairs behind him. My knuckles hurt but the adrenaline is dulling the feeling. Atsuko and I walk back to our cars arm in arm and in silence.

Atsuko follows me back to my place, walking me inside the front door. Akmal stands up from the couch when he sees me, and then looks at Atsuko with a questioning expression.

"I'll see you later, okay?" Atsuko's soft whisper against my ear only puts Akmal on high alert at something being wrong. When she exits, I shut the door quietly and lock it behind her.

Akmal turns me around, gently but firmly grabs my right hand and brings it up to his face. "What happened?" His eyes are boring into my knuckles as they start to redden up.

"It wasn't anything important."

"It was important enough for you to throw a fucking punch."

Sighing and leaning into his chest, Akmal embraces me tightly, rubbing my back in soothing circles. I love this. I love his calm energy, especially when I don't feel calm on the inside. My gut is still churning at meeting Roman randomly after over a decade apart.

"Tell me what's wrong." Akmal's whisper makes me hold him tighter.

"I ran into one of my exes -" Akmal's body tenses up and it feels like he's trying to break our embrace but I only hold him tighter. "-but I handled it. I didn't want to see that fucker's face. I'm sure he'll be hiding out for a while until he's healed up, he's always been vain like that."

With a sigh, Akmal continues to hold me until my heart settles back into something warm, happy and content.

Chapter Twenty-Six

VERO

We visited Akmal's parents today for lunch. It was nice and hectic as usual. I swear they are the hub for all Malaysians in the area. I don't know if it's something I ate but I don't feel so good.

"We're almost home, hold on for me okay?"

We make it back without any incident and after a good nap, I feel a whole lot better. I'm going to have to remember what I ate to make sure I avoid it the next time I'm over there.

Akmal must have finished up his edits during my nap because I find him sitting on the floor with his laptop on the coffee table and a game on the screen.

"Hey, baby."

"Hey! Are you feeling any better?"

"Yeah, that nap helped a lot. I must have eaten something that didn't agree with me. Can you help me keep an eye out the next time we have lunch with your parents? I'm not sure which plate it was."

"Yeah, yeah, of course. I'll call them and let them know." Plopping down next to him, I snuggle his arm and watch him play. He has his headset on and I think I can hear Mat's voice.

Giving my husband a peck on the cheek, I get up to go call Atsuko since the boys are busy. It rings twice before she picks up.

"I'm so glad you called. I was starting to get a little bored watching Mat talk to your man on that game. They're really into it today."

"What are you up to, chica?"

"Nothing much, Mat and I had the conversation about me helping out with the business. I think ... I think I'm just going to go for it. I'm going to put in my two weeks at the makeup counter soon."

Walking back into the bedroom, I lie on my back and just stare at the picture sitting on our night stand. The luncheon with the in-laws was also for them to give us the wedding pictures and holy hell there were a lot of them. Figures since it felt like we sat on that throne all damn day.

"I'm so glad you're coming on. I need you to help calm me down if I'm about to get on some of the female clients when they're acting the way they shouldn't."

"Pfft. You and I both. Make sure you keep me in check because sometimes my fist speaks first and I ask questions later." We both laugh because it's so damn true. You can take the girl out of the hood, but you can't take the hood out of the girl.

"What are you doing tomorrow?"

"Nothing I guess. Hmm, maybe I should turn in my two weeks tomorrow?"

"Yeah, why not? The sooner the better. There's really no difference in waiting."

"You're right."

"Hey, you want to hang at Big Burger like old times?" That sounds like a damn excellent plan. I love the retro feel of that place. Atsuko and I used to hang out there at least every other week when we still lived together. Has it really been that long?

"Hell yeah! Type up that notice girl, we'll drop that shit off then head over to Big Burger."

"Sounds good. See you then."

"See you then." We hang up and I'm feeling really good. I'm excited to have another girl date with Atsuko. I mean, I love hanging out with Akmal, getting bent into a pretzel and pounded into, but girl time is important too. Keeps my mind on the straight and narrow when my thoughts about stupid stuff get chaotic.

Tossing my phone onto the mattress, I get up from the bed and start walking towards the kitchen. Might as well find a snack to eat if I'm going to sit and watch Akmal play video games. He's so cute though, I have no reason to complain. Other women would kill to keep their men home. I really am lucky in that sense.

When the coolness of the fridge hits me, I take in a deep breath. That feels good. But what doesn't feel good is the fact that the fridge is almost empty. Do two people really go through food that quickly?

"Hey babe, I'm going to go grocery shopping before it gets dark. We're low on food."

"Alright, just grab my credit card from my wallet." A man after my own heart. I love this guy.

A quick shower, getting redressed into comfy clothes and a hair bun later I'm giving Akmal a kiss on the cheek before heading out.

AKMAL

After helping Vero put away the groceries, we join each other on the floor. I could game on the kitchen table, but I find the couch makes a nicer backrest. Plus the coffee table is the perfect height. Vero went through a good handful of snacks she brought home and is now dozing off with her head on my lap as I carefully lean into the game with Mat.

"Someone behind you."

"Shit, I see him."

"How are you and Vero doing?"

"Good, real good. I would say I should have married earlier if I knew it would be like this but then it wouldn't have been with Vero."

"Yeah, I feel the same way. Had to snatch her up before someone else did."

"I feel you. Vero is it for me. Just seeing some guy come in at her work looking at her tits made me want to start going on a killing spree." Mat laughs as we continue to shoot the enemy and creep along the trees to find a new hiding spot.

The sound of characters dying makes me do a quick check on the mini map. Mat's still in.

"I understand man. That's why the gym is good for me. It gets out my rage, you know? You're always welcome to join me."

"That's cool, I might. But I've also found better ways to take my frustrations out."

"Yeah?" I take down three guys and start changing out my long range weapons for short ones as I take my character into an abandoned house. My mind floats back to the other day...

I need to knock my wife up. Taking her pills away is too much, maybe crossing the line. We're too early in our relationship for that. She'll kill me.

My fingers glide across the phone's keyboard as I start researching the rate of failure for oral contraceptives. I don't like what I'm reading and pulling up, but a line catches my eye.

"Oral contraceptive pills on the other hand have a failure rate of 0.1%, this means that 1 woman out of 1000..." Shit, I can do this.

I've watched Vero and her routines closely but I've never paid attention to the time she takes her pill. That's going to change. That's going to change right the fuck now.

Maybe if I keep her busy, it will throw her schedule off and increase the probability rate. Yes. Sounds like the perfect plan.

The sound of gunshots nearby brings me back to the present, my eyes scanning the screen for any potential threats near me.

"Yeah." I've been fucking her every chance I get, which is never a hardship to begin with. Her pussy just greedily takes everything I give her.

"Care to share, my friend?" Hiding my character behind a dark wall, I take a peek down to make sure my wife is sleeping. She is judging by the slow breathing and feeling of deadweight on my legs right now.

"So, you see, Vero likes to be a brat sometimes." Lately, it seems like all the time. I glance back down at her again. Still asleep.

"What do you mean?"

"Something about her man. She riles me up and I think she does it on purpose. Once I caught on, I started testing my theory by making her take small punishments."

I can hear gunshots from Mat's side.

"What do you mean punishments? Like you're spanking her or something?"

"Among other things." We both laugh and continue to take down a few on the other team. Somehow I run into Mat's character and we start to buddy up on the screen.

He whistles into the mic and I'm glad I'm on a headset. That shit would have woken Vero up.

"She like it?"

"Shit, more than like it man. That girl almost begs for it. She keeps trying to make me cum in her mouth but I've been trying my damndest to put a baby in her."

"Yeah? Already?"

"Fuck yes. I'm going to keep her pregnant. Makes me fucking hot just thinking about it."

"Fuck, maybe I should knock up Atsuko too." This statement is said in a whisper, she must not be too far away. He clears his throat. She must have just walked by. I'm laughing as light as I can so I don't jostle my sleeping beauty that much.

"Damn, now you got me thinking Akmal. My dick is hard. Last game."

"You got it bro. Last game."

Chapter Twenty-Seven

VERO

Atsuko and I carpooled in her vehicle to make it easier on our girl date. I went in with her to drop off her notice. They didn't even give a rat's ass since the new girl apparently is monopolizing everyone's hours anyway. She's young and she's ambitious. It's good that Atsuko is leaving this junk for the new generation. You don't want to compete with that.

Pulling up on Big Burger, it's just how I remembered. Like a flash to the fifties when you open the doors. Atsuko and I sit at our usual table and some of the waitresses still remember us.

"I feel like it was just yesterday when Mat brought me here."

"I know what you mean. Feels like just yesterday I was trying to get the attention of your photographer at the car show. The fool wouldn't even give me a sideways glance no matter how much I tried to push the girls into his face."

We laugh and relax with each other, ordering our usual. Well, maybe a little extra for me. I haven't had a shake in a while and it's sounding real good today.

"Something is up with Mat this morning."

"Yeah?"

"I mean, we always fuck like rabbits, but it's just something extra. I can't put my finger on it."

"If he's not holding out, then you have nothing to worry about. Maybe he's just feeling for a little extra. Guys are like that."

"Is your guy like that?"

"I mean, I'm Akmal's first so it's not like I have anything else to compare to in regards to him but yeah, we're fucking like the world's ending."

The waitress is laughing as she puts our food on the table. They know how we are, we have no filters and we can get a little loud when the conversation gets rolling.

"That's good right? He was such a shy guy to begin with."

"Yeah, it's like something snapped. Well, I take that back, we were teasing a whole lot before the wedding so maybe something happened along the way." We giggle at that because we both know how bad I can get when I want some.

Atsuko throws a fry at me, the bitch. "You're so bad! That poor boy never stood a chance and now you've turned him into a nympho."

Opening my milkshake, I dip the fries in and take a bite. "No no no. Let's not get carried away. Nymphos will bang anything on two legs. Akmal just wants to bang *this* cooch." I smile as I take another bite of fries dipped in milkshake.

"You're right. Akmal is loyal. You got yourself a good one babe. Keep him."

Opening my burger wrapper, I dip the burger into my shake and take a bite out of that too. This shit is so good, who knew? I'm halfway through my burger when I notice Atsuko staring at me with a fry halfway to her mouth.

Making sure to chew what I have in my mouth, I wipe my lips before asking, "What?"

"When the hell did you start eating like that?"

"Like what?"

"I mean, you've always dunked your fries, but your burger?" Taking another large bite, I chew and think over what she said. Have I ever dipped my burger before?

Swallowing, I take a huge gulp of my shake before answering. "I guess you're right. Tastes fucking good though, you should try it."

"Nah, I'm good."

We eat in silence for a few moments and I realize I already polished off my burger. Has it always been that small? Grabbing a few fries at once, I shove it into my mouth and savor the salty flavor.

"Vero." Damn, I'm halfway through my fries. Maybe the shake will fill me up.

"Huh?" Dusting my fingers off with my napkin as I finish my last fry, I look up at Atsuko. She's only halfway through her meal. When did she get so slow?

"Babe...are you-"

Sucking on my shake, the sweetness is such a nice contrast to the salty flavor of the fries. Good thing I ate that last. Yum.

"Vero, are you pregnant?"

"Pfft, not possible. I'm still on the pill. Akmal hasn't mentioned wanting to start so I just kept taking it."

"I guess you're right. You want to drive by and get a test just in case?" Finishing my shake, I nod my head as I wipe the sweetness from my lips.

"Sure, but it will probably just be a waste of time and money. Why not though?"

Atsuko finishes off her meal as I hit up the restroom. We exit Big Burger and drive by a nearby drug store to pick up some pregnancy tests.

"Oh my god, there are so many." Atsuko and I are just standing in the aisle like a bunch of fools staring at these different boxes. Why do you need so many different kinds if they're all doing the same damn thing?

"Shit, this is harder than I thought. Oh! But look at this one, it's cheaper because it's a box of two. What am I going to do with the other one though?"

Atsuko looks at the box in my hand and shrugs. "I can take one with you if you want. That way we use up the sticks and we're both doing it together."

I laugh because that's just like Atsuko. Why the hell not? YOLO. It's not like the stick is going to change anything. We ring up the box together and split the cost. Supposedly this one will actually have words that show up instead of lines. Good, that way it's super clear and no one can be confused about what they're reading.

We head back to Atsuko's place because my car is parked there. Mat and Akmal went to the gym and were planning on doing whatever guy stuff they do while Atsuko and I had our girl time so the place is empty when we arrive. Perfect for the shit we're about to do. Don't want to freak the guys out or anything over a silly test.

Dropping off our purses on the kitchen table, we grab the box and both head to the restroom. Atsuko opens her medicine cabinet to make more counter space around the sink. It wasn't like it was that full to begin with, but whatever floats her boat.

"Alright, so the directions say that we're literally going to pee on this thing." Atsuko is opening the folded pamphlet and looking at it front and back. There sure are a lot of words for such a 'simple' test.

"Okay, I can do that." Atsuko's restroom smells nice, like something floral. I'm going to have to ask her what she uses so I can use it in our restroom too.

"It says the best pee is probably in the morning but whatever. Let's do this." She hands me one stick while she takes the other. We both look at each other and laugh while we get out of our bottoms.

Both half naked we take turns squatting over the toilet and peeing on the stupid thing. We're laughing after we're done when we realized we didn't have to remove our bottoms completely. This shit is way out of our league.

Resituating our clothing and washing our hands, we leave the sticks on the sink counter - Atsuko's on the left, mine on the right - before we go chill on the couch and watch some TV. The pamphlet said to give it a few minutes but we gave it about ten just in case. There wasn't anything else we really needed to know, so the paper got tossed in the trash right before we left the restroom.

When the alarm goes off on my phone, we both get up and go look at our sticks. Laughing when we get there, we make sure to remind each other which belongs to whom.

Looking at each other, trying to smother a grin at the craziness of it all, we both pick it up at the same time and try to read the little writing that shows up in the little window.

"Well..."

"Yeah."

We both look at each other before putting the sticks back down.

Chapter Twenty-Eight

VERO

I'm kind of scared, I'm not going to lie. Atsuko and I were sitting around trying to figure out what happened. Leaving her house before Mat gets there, I'm trying to take my time in getting home myself.

I stopped at a random parking lot to look this shit up on my phone. I'm probably worrying about nothing because that junk gets wrong all the time, right? I've heard the stories.

Bringing up my phone's browser, I start typing in the failure rate of birth control pills. It doesn't seem too bad. 0.1% chance. I keep scrolling and start to give up because all the information is about the same.

Staring out my front windshield, I watch as people walk by trying to find their cars. I'm getting kind of hungry. I wonder if this store sells food too? But cold food would probably go bad by the time I get done shopping and looking up this shit. Ain't nobody got time for that.

Bringing my phone back up, I start to look up my specific brand of oral contraceptives. I remember it changing recently, I think. Would this have anything to do with it? Eh, it's a long shot, but I'll check it out anyway while I'm here.

Different news feeds start popping up on the search and I start browsing through some of them. Huh, it seems like the formula was different from the other brand it replaced. I don't know if this is good or bad, I mean, I don't feel any different.

The more I read, the more I'm finding that there has been an increase in failure rate among this specific brand. Going back to the previous few articles I've read, I'm noticing a trend I didn't see the first time around.

They all date a few months back.

Turning my phone off, I let all I've learned soak in before starting the car back up and driving home.

When I walk through the front door, I can hear the sound of the shower going. Akmal must be in there. Dropping my purse off and hanging my keys up, I open the freezer and let the cool air hit my face. Opening my eyes, I see rows of ice cream tubs and I want to squeal. Akmal really is the best husband ever.

Grabbing one, and a spoon out of the kitchen drawer, I plant my ass on the couch and turn on some TV. The first bite of ice cream hits me in the right place. Holy hell, what flavor is this? Lifting the carton up, it says Rocky Road. I've had this before but it never tasted like this. Why does it taste so damn good?

I must be moaning too loudly because I didn't even hear Akmal get out of the shower and walk into the room. He leans over the back of the couch and gives me a kiss on the cheek. Sweet, sweet man.

"Hey, did you have fun with Atsuko?" He smells so clean, so masculine. He may even smell more delicious than this damn ice cream I'm shoveling into my mouth right now. My eyes track his movements and muscles as he parades himself to the refrigerator. He's only in shorts and that delectable ass of his is bending over for my viewing pleasure.

"Mmmhmmm."

I'm licking the spoon more than I should as I watch him grab a bottle of water and lift it up to drink. The way his Adam's apple bobs and the way his biceps flex makes me kind of needy. But when am I ever *not* needy around this man? I am one lucky son of a -

The couch jostles a little as Akmal sits down right next to me, placing the bottle onto the coffee table and throwing his arm over the back of the couch. The way his hair kind of falls over his eyes is sexy as hell, I never noticed it before. Akmal pushes his hair back before we hear his phone ring from somewhere in the back.

I watch as he gets up and round the couch while shoveling another mouthful of rocky road in. My body is missing his warmth already. I shouldn't eat this all too quickly. Ice cream will start becoming scarce before I want it to. Akmal doesn't really eat any I've noticed, so I've just been spooning it to my heart's content rather than putting scoops of it in a bowl.

Getting up, I toss the spoon into the sink and close the carton back up before placing it back into the freezer. I need to text Atsuko my findings about that birth control pill. We used to be on the same brand, I wonder if her doctor changed hers too?

Doing just that, I lean over the arm of the couch to grab my phone, staying in that position as I quickly forward her the links to the articles I read.

> **Vero:** Hey check this shit out.
>
> **Atsuko:** Okay, what's up?
>
> **Vero:** My birth control brand got changed a while back, did yours?
>
> **Atsuko:** You know, I never really paid attention. I have no fucking clue.
>
> **Vero:** Well, check this shit out because the brand I got changed to has some issues. It's not working for some women.
>
> **Atsuko:** Yeah? I better look.

I can hear Akmal's voice getting closer and closer by the increase in sound.

"Yeah, she got home not too long ago." Akmal walks by and slaps my ass since it's still hanging over the arm of the couch. Good thing he didn't look over my shoulder as I discreetly and nonchalantly try to talk to my BFF about the issue on hand.

Vero: Hey did you get rid of the tests?

Atsuko: Yeah, I put some toilet paper over it too.

Vero: Okay, good. The boys don't need to know yet until we know what the hell is going on.

Atsuko: You got that right.

Atsuko: Are you scared, Vero?

Vero: I don't know if I should be yet. I mean, that shit gets wrong all the time right?

Atsuko: Yeah, I guess...

"Wait, what? Say that one more time, I don't think I heard you right the first time." I black out my screen when I hear Akmal right next to me. I'm not ready to talk about this yet. I need to find out more information first before I start throwing around false information. Plus there's no point in worrying about something you're not sure of yet.

Straightening up, I smooth down my clothes and look at Akmal who hasn't moved an inch from where he's standing - a foot away from me.

"Yeah, I'll call you back." He's staring at me and I don't know why. I try to give him a smile.

"Is everything okay?"

"Yeah, everything's fine. Did you have a good time with Atsuko today? Do anything interesting?"

"I always have fun with my BFF. We didn't do much, just went to eat at Big Burgers and hung out."

He's staring at me and I'm starting to feel like a mouse under a microscope. What was he and Mat talking about? It had to be Mat, no one else really calls him. All his photography stuff is handled via emails and messenger online.

"Hmmm. You guys eat a good meal then?"

"Yes, it was absolutely delicious as usual. The food went way too fast, they need to make bigger sizes for their combos."

"Is that right?"

Akmal's phone rings again and I watch as he connects it without taking his eyes off me. My hands are starting to get clammy from the tension in this room. Is it getting hot in here?

"Yeah." His eyes are scanning my face, but his expression is still so blank. I'm on pins and needles now. What is going on?

"Thanks for letting me know. I'll call you back." Akmal hangs up and tosses his cell phone onto the couch behind me, the move startling me with how abrupt it is.

"So, nothing else happened today on your date with Atsuko?"

"Not really, we just kind of hung out at her place for a little."

He stares at me, I stare at him. The tension in the room amps up tenfold but I'm not one to back down from a challenge or break first. No no no. We were being good girls. Yup. Mmmhmm.

"Vero."

"Akmal."

"Fucking hell." Wait, what? "Vero, do you need to tell me something?"

"Nooo. Why would I?" Dammit, why am I like this?

"No?"

"Nope." I make the 'p' pop for emphasis because I'm feeling a little extra right now. He needs to get off my back.

"No." He's repeating me but it's coming out like a low whisper. I can tell he's trying to suppress a grin and it's making me try to suppress my grin. Challenge accepted fucker.

But when he takes the last couple of steps towards me with dark hunger in his eyes, I gulp and start to feel like a little chicken. When his scent surrounds me, my eyes flutter a bit and I have to mentally slap myself to stand strong against his sexy ass ways.

What do they say about facing a predator? Don't look away. *Alright Vero, come on girl, don't look away.*

We're basically toe to toe. He leans in a little and I inadvertently lean back a little, my ass on the arm of the couch.

His hand shoots out and grabs the back of my neck as he leans in, putting his cheek against mine. "Are you lying to me, Vero?" The octaves of his voice have gone so low I can feel the timber of it down to my core. Oh my god. *Stand your ground!*

"N-no."

He starts kissing the crook of my neck, his facial hair scraping my skin and making it prickle. When his tongue starts to lick and his lips start to suck and nip, my legs get a little weak. He's sucking hard now and it makes my nipples perk up, rubbing against the lace of my bra. The room is getting hotter because I swear I'm sweating between my tits right now from how he has me cornered.

He gives me another hard suck to the point of teetering on pain then proceeds to lave at the spot with the flat of his tongue, soothing it away and making me sigh. "Did you go to the store with Atsuko today?" His tongue is trailing up my jaw until he captures my mouth in his, invading it, owning it. He's making my brain foggy. He's playing me like a damn fiddle.

"What does that matter?" I manage to say between our lips colliding. Oh dear lord, Akmal growls into my mouth and starts plundering it with full force, dominating my movements with his. I can only go along for the ride as I find myself lost in what he's doing to me. Our eyes are still open as we stare at each other, the tension in the room so thick you can cut it with a knife.

His hands are moving in quick succession while his mouth continues to ravish mine. Our teeth hitting each other at times from how rough our movements have become. My body is being forced into different positions and the cool air coming between us now and again tells me he's been stripping me like a damn magician.

How he got me naked except for my bra this fast, I have no idea. This man is far from the virgin I remember. He pulls the soft lace cup of my bra down and fists my hair, tilting my head back and taking my nipple into his mouth.

Oh, but he's not in a playing mood today, no. A suck, a lick and a nip later, he grabs my ass and hefts me up. My legs automatically wrap around him to prevent me from falling, trapping his hard cock between us. His head comes forward to take my other nipple in his mouth as he walks us somewhere. With my arms wrapped around his shoulders and my fingers threading through his hair, my mouth is gaping open from how hard he's attacking it. With each step he takes, the hard tip of his cock behind his clothes rubs against my clit and wet pussy lips, making us glide against each other, wetting the fabric between us.

My back hits a wall and it almost knocks the air out of me. Akmal quickly pulls his shorts down and shoves his cock all the way in with one hard stroke.

"Vero -" *Thrust* "Did you" *Thrust* "go to the store today?" *Thrust thrust.*

I'm speechless with how hard he's pounding into me. He's hitting things he hasn't hit before with his enthusiasm. I open my mouth to say something but I can't do anything else but gasp and moan like a wanton ho.

His hands grip my ass even harder with my non-answer and Akmal starts to force my hips against him every time he pounds into me.

"You're such a little liar, Vero." My pussy is already fluttering with everything that's happened. "Why do you need to be brat all the time?"

Oh my god. Am I expected to answer that right now? How fucking rude of him to ask! Oh shit, I can feel my body tensing, the sensations are getting higher.

"Is it because you want me to fuck you? Is that it?" Oh fuck, what is he doing with his hips? He's twisting it somehow. *Oh dear god.*

"Is it because you like to get punished for being a bad little girl?" Yes! Hell yes! But I can't tell him that because...because -

I cry out as one of his twisted grinds hits me in the right spot and I'm seeing fucking stars as my body tightens and almost wants to convulse. My pussy is clenching around his cock and a few more thrusts later - banging my head against the damn wall - Akmal is groaning into my chest, biting me right under my collarbone.

The feeling of his cock spurting cum inside me makes me ride waves after falling off the climax cliff. It's glorious and I'm panting. Akmal pulls us away from the wall and lowers us ungracefully onto the carpeted floor when he just lies on top of me, trying to catch his breath.

My hands are petting him and rubbing his back, the dampness of his skin making my hands stick a bit. Akmal is nuzzling my breasts and kissing them as he sneaks in, "I know what you did, Vero."

Chapter Twenty-Nine

AKMAL

I'm flabbergasted at the fact that she continues to deny it. Or at least deny that it's a plausibility. She is so damn stubborn sometimes. We've been insatiable with each other, how can it not be a possibility. I punished her again last night in our bedroom, restraining her when she started fighting against me thinking it would make me stop. I would never stop, not with my wife. She gets like this when conversations are about to escalate into unnecessary arguments. I don't know if she gets a kick out of it or what but I'm starting to read her better and better.

She slept so soundly, not noticing the way I caressed her skin under the moonlight that spilled into the bedroom window. She fought so hard and so long that by the time I was able to get her little spitfire rage out of her system, she fell asleep with my cum leaking out of her - butt naked. That's alright, I love her like this. She's so damn soft and I can't stop myself from rubbing against her from behind as we lie together in bed. She didn't even wake up when I entered her again, only squirming and moaning in her sleep. It was hard going slow when all we seem to be used to these days is fast and hard.

The morning light woke me early. There's a lot on my mind and things need to get done. I wasn't able to rouse Vero until almost noon. We don't have anything booked for the next couple of days so I head to the kitchen to make her breakfast when I hear her stirring in bed. The pan is sizzling with the ingredients I prepared beforehand.

"Good morning, baby." There she is. Even like this, she's the most beautiful woman I've ever seen. The bruises and hickies on her body fill me with a sense of pride. She smells like she's been having sex all night - which is the damn truth, I made sure of it.

"Eat, get dressed. We're heading out today."

She blinks a few times but is still too groggy to argue. Good. I planned it that way. Heading to the bedroom, I grab some of her looser clothes and place them on the bed for her. When I enter the kitchen again, she's just finishing up her small omelette.

"Drink some water." She does as she's told with wide eyes.

The moment she puts the cup down is the moment I grab her and carry her bridal style, depositing her into the restroom and tapping her ass to hurry up. I'm already dressed and waiting by the time she's done with her shower.

She eyes the clothes skeptically, giving me a sideways glance. I'm not playing today and my face surely shows it because she doesn't say a word as she puts them on.

The drive to our destination is quiet, but without the tension that was around us yesterday. Vero is easy to side-track when she gets fired up, I've been using it to my advantage and now it's time to get this done right.

Putting the car in park, I quickly get out and open her passenger door. Gripping her hand tightly, I drag her through the double glass doors and straight to the front desk.

"Do you have an appointment?"

"Yes, with Doctor Garcia at 1:30pm."

"Ah, the OBGYN." The receptionist types into her computer for a good second before turning back to us and telling us to have a seat.

Sitting down, I pull Vero onto my lap.

"Akmal!"

"Shh. This is a doctor's office."

"I can't believe you."

"You should. We're here."

"We don't need to -"

"Akmal! Good to see you! How is your family? This must be your wife, congratulations. Your mother has been spreading the news about your nuptials. She's very proud."

"You know how she is. This is Vero. Vero, this is Doctor Garcia, a family friend who was kind enough to give us an appointment quickly."

I can see my wife side eyeing me but it makes no difference. We're already here. Leading us to the back, my wife grips my arm firmly.

Once we're in the designated private room, Doctor Garcia hands Vero a urine cup and proceeds to tell her to take her clothes off for a pap smear right after. It was a bit difficult once the good doctor left the room, but I was able to convince her to do what she needed to do. Vero can be strong willed but yields with the right methods.

Vero comes back into the room without the urine cup and is avoiding my eyes as I stare at her movements. It's a good thing she didn't wear her signature red lipstick today. My eyes blaze with the puffy way her lips are looking right now, the evidence of what I had to do. When her eyes find mine, they're filled with fire and it makes my cock twitch.

The doctor comes in before we can settle our silent dispute and tells me what I already know.

"Congratulations! You're pregnant!"

Vero is looking at me with a shocked expression and I feel my smile start to creep up my lips.

VERO

"Vero! It was so sad!" Atsuko's voice is getting emotionally high, I wish I could give her a hug right now.

"I mean, what did he do when he found the sticks in the trash can?" It's been a couple of days before I could find some private time to call my BFF about my news.

"He confronted me and asked me if I was pregnant. You should have seen him Vero. The hopeful look on his face." Atsuko's stick was negative while mine was positive that fateful day. When she told me she got rid of the evidence, I didn't think she'd do such a bad job at it. I can't believe she just threw that shit in the trash can. She could have dumped the evidence in a dumpster or something. But I love her and I really feel for her right now.

"I told him it wasn't mine and it almost broke my heart seeing his face crumple. I didn't even know he was wanting to try for a baby, or else I wouldn't have been taking the pills." I can hear Atsuko sniffing on the phone. It must have hit Mat pretty hard for her to react like this.

"Well, you know men. They're not that great in communication. Especially our guys, seeing as how we're their first real relationship."

"I know, I know. But I felt like my heart was caving in with how much it hurt him. I heard him on the phone with someone while we were giving each other space. I didn't know what else to do or say to him." The sound of Atsuko blowing her nose comes clearly over the phone.

"So that's how Akmal knew..."

"Sorry, but I can't lie to Mat. Not when he looked like that. I held him for the rest of the night after we made love. He didn't talk much."

"No need to apologize, I mean it was going to come to light anyway right?" Akmal, caveman he is, made sure it came out to light with a second opinion via an OBGYN. I should be mad with how he dragged me there without my permission, but he's been on cloud nine since the news. He even started rummaging through my things and chucking out all my birth control pills. It's not like they worked anyway.

Wait a minute.

"Atsuko."

"Yeah?"

"Do me a favor and don't ask questions okay?"

"Alright."

"I'll pick you up in thirty minutes." The boys have a small photoshoot today, so they'll be out for a little bit. We can sneak this in.

By the time I drive up to Atsuko's place, she's already walked out to the parking lot to meet me.

"What's happening?"

"You'll find out in a bit." Tires squealing, we head to the last place Akmal took me. Doctor Garcia really is a family friend and was kind enough to sneak Atsuko in for a quick appointment.

"This might be a waste of time, Vero. The stick gave me a negative." My best friend's eyes are still a little pink from the crying jag she had earlier with our phone conversation.

"Then what would it hurt? It won't change a thing. But I mean, I just remembered the fact that you're using the same damn brand of birth control as me right? I saw it at your house the last time I was there. Just do it girl. Do it for Mat." Her eyes tear up a little again at the mention of his name as she nods her head.

Once she's done peeing in the cup, we wait together in the private room, holding hands. Atsuko is nervous and I'm nervous for her. When the door opens up, we both hold our breaths.

"Congratulations! You are going to be a mother!" Atsuko breaks down and cries openly and loudly while I pet her back. "It's okay, sometimes it depends on your levels of hCG and the time of day you pee on the stick. But your levels must be high enough now for it to be detected. Congratulations again."

Atsuko is almost ugly crying at this point against my shoulder. I thank Doctor Garcia who exits the room with a sympathetic smile.

Epilogue

VERO

Akmal was adamant that we have a whole damn family luncheon for this thing. I'm nervous as hell, but excited at the same time. My mother, being the nosey woman she is, kept asking what this was about when I called her the other day to invite her. It took a lot of persuading but she finally agreed to bring everyone over. Stubborn woman.

Akmal was so excited about this whole thing, he invited Mat and Atsuko too since they're basically family. I haven't talked to Atsuko since the last time; Akmal has been so busy going over things we need to rearrange and such to make room for the baby. He's more into this than I am and I'm pretty into it since I'm the damn mother.

Placing my hand over my flat stomach, I smile at the thought of a life growing in there. It's so surreal. Akmal pulls up in front of his parents' house and is smiling at me from the driver's side. He's so damn happy that I can't help but be overly happy with him. Reading up on first time pregnancies, I did get nervous when google kept telling me that I'm an older mother and at higher risk for issues. Akmal kept reassuring me and went out to get all the prenatal vitamins and healthy food I would need for a balanced meal. I still sneak in ice cream, he's not taking that shit away from me.

Helping me out of the passenger side, we walk hand and hand to the front door where Akmal's mother is already waiting with her hands on her hips. Looking at her hijab, I'm reminded of our wedding day. It feels like it's been a million years ago and only yesterday. Is it always going to feel like this with Akmal? I wouldn't have it any other way. He's filled my life in ways I never could have imagined. Who knew Vero Hernandez was made for the married life?

"Akmal! You need to visit more huh. Why are you hiding away my daughter-in-law?"

"Ibu, I'm not hiding away your daughter-in-law."

"I know you are lying, but it's okay. You're here now. I called Hasanah and Sakinah, they are already here. Come come."

We haven't even greeted everyone yet when I hear my parents and Fabian not far behind us. I'm surprised I didn't hear his car. They must have taken my parent's vehicle. Mat and Atsuko follow a few minutes shortly after and that makes the whole gang.

"Sit down, sit down. Makan, Makan. We can eat while Akmal tells us what he needs to tell us. There is enough food for everyone!" Akmal's mother is admirable with her hospitality. I'm going to have to start picking up some tips and tricks since Akmal literally told me he's going to keep me knocked up, the brute.

The seating arrangement is similar to the last time we had a family luncheon, the parents in one circle and everyone else in another but the two main couples close enough to each other. As we start eating, a weird tension is shimmering between Fabian and Sakinah. I can't put my finger on whether it is from annoyance or hate. But the looks Sakinah shoots his way is scary. The lip curl doesn't help either, she hides it quickly before anyone else around her notices. Fabian being Fabian gives her a grin but there's something else there in his eyes that I can't read from this angle. What happened between those two?

Once most of us are done eating and some plates are down, Akmal clears his throat to get everyone's attention. "Everyone!" The room goes quiet and my cheeks feel flushed from the attention. I don't even know why I'm embarrassed, I shouldn't be.

"Vero is pregnant!" The roar that goes up is almost deafening, most of it coming from the mothers. Congratulations go around and everyone is in a light mood. Backs are being slapped and everyone's getting side hugs.

It takes a good while before everyone settles down but they do quickly when Atsuko's soft voice floats in the air. "Um, I have something to say too." Everyone still has smiles on their faces as they all turn to give her their attention. I smile at her encouragingly when she casts her gaze to me, nervousness in her eyes. *Come on girl, you got this.*

"I'm pregnant too." Mat almost topples her over when he slams himself into her in an embrace and the living room goes into another uproar that will probably have the neighbors calling the cops.

SAKINAH

Everyone is excited over the news of Atsuko and Vero's pregnancies. I am too but my family can be a bit much, so I slip away out the back to get a little bit of fresh air. My parents had called me in for this luncheon, but I need to head back to the university after this.

The crisp air outside always lightens the load I feel on my mind. I'm taking on a lot but I can do it. I need to do it. I want to start becoming independent as soon as I can and start living life. At twenty-five, my mother has been pushing me to get married but I think I need to find myself first.

Malaysian culture can feel so oppressive sometimes. I wonder what it would be like to be like the other westernized girls out there. Girls like Vero are comfortable in their own skin and own themselves, moving with an air of confidence.

Who am I?

"Sakinah." I internally groan when I hear his voice. He couldn't just give me a minute alone, could he? I thought we already established that this friendship thing isn't going to work out.

"Fabian."

"What are you doing out here? Were you waiting for me?" This guy.

"Don't be perasan la. Don't flatter yourself, Fabian. Can't a girl just come out for some fresh air? Not everything revolves around you." I can see him grinning to the side of me but I refuse to give him my full attention. That's exactly what he wants. Fabian is a man who looks like he always gets what he wants. Well, tough luck.

I decide to turn a little bit more away from him, hinting to him that I really don't want to put up with his shit right now when his tall, hard body moves me towards the side of the house farther away from the backdoor.

His front is to my back and my hands become locked in his grip as he brings them up to either side of my face, our fingers intertwined like the lovers *we are not.*

"What are you doing?" I don't mean to sound like I have an attitude but I am not feeling this crap right now.

"Sakinah. I can't stop thinking about you."

"You mean about that fucking slap to your face. It's supposed to tell you to leave me the hell alone." The masculine chuckle by my ear makes me internally shiver, but I try to remain stoic. That's just what he wants from me, a reaction. He can't stand the fact that I'm not throwing myself all over him.

The thought of other girls doing this with him amps up my anger again, overshadowing whatever feelings he was starting to evoke in me while we're in this compromised position.

"So you think about it too, huh? I have to say, my cock hasn't gotten that hard in a while, Sakinah."

"Walao eh, oh my god." This guy. I'm disgusted and turned on at the same time. What is wrong with me?

I try to buck my body to get him off me but it only makes him grind his crotch against my ass. My face is flaming and now I'm glad I'm facing the wall, so he can't see the effect he really does have on me. It's starting to get hot underneath my clothes with the way his body heat is consuming me like a damn inferno. A dangerous inferno.

"Get off me Fabian."

"Go out with me Sakinah."

"I thought we were trying to be friends."

"Friends can still go out. Come on."

"Get off me." He spins me around and my mind is still trying to catch up with the movement when his mouth lands on mine again. Fuck. This guy keeps stealing kisses from me and I hate the fact that I love it. The forbidden nature of it all only serves to make it hotter than it should be. Our lips glide for a few seconds and I come to my senses, biting his bottom lip, making him hiss and step away.

I quickly escape the sexual tension by slipping back through the back door and into the living room where everyone is still abuzz about whether the women will have boy or girl babies.

Author's Note

Why is Fabian and Sakinah's potential relationship forbidden when they're technically not related? Well, an alpha reader [for the Malaysian side] has informed me that once you are married into the family, you are not allowed to have any sort of relations of that kind. It is not allowed and it is very much frowned upon.

What does this mean for our couple? It could mean many things. Middle sister Sakinah is the most rebellious of the girls in Akmal's family. She wishes to be more independent and westernized like Vero, as you see in this epilogue.

But you know what they say: be careful what you ask for because you just might get it.

This will lead to dramatic changes, ones she will have to learn to accept or she will have to learn to deny the love that grows between herself and Fabian.

Who would you choose? Family or love?

Playlist

Christina Aguilera - Lord Have Mercy on Me
Postmodern Jukebox - All About That Bass
Etta James - At Last
NOTD, Shy Martin - Keep You Mine (Acoustic)
Christina Aguilera - Nasty Naughty Boy
John Legend - All of Me
Beyonce - Halo
Nina Simone - I Put a Spell on You
Luis Fonsi - Despacito ft. Daddy Yankee
Christina Aguilera - Save Me From Myself
Imelda May - It's Good To Be Alive
Jencarlos Canela - Bajito ft. Kymani Marley

If you get your kicks in a magical manner, order toys from websites like bad dragon, and prefer your monsters *in* your bed instead of *under* them, then Y. D. is your girl.

Writing everything from spicy dark fantasy to fluffier-than-a-cool-marshmallow romance, Y.D. La Mar has her fingers in all sorts of man-meat pie, and the sky is the limit. Somehow, this magical mistress manages to balance her spicy author life with her responsibilities as a mom, a wife, and a resident of Sin City—*oh, irony, you've felled me.*

When the world is full of black-and-white, Y.D. plays in the grey zones, spending her time creating new ways to shock and awe her editor, as well as her readers.

Follow Me!

Want updates and sneak peeks?

Sign up for my newsletter!

Also by YD La Mar

STREET ARRHYTHMIA TRILOGY

The Scent of Jasmine

For The Love of Import & Blood

To The Beat of The Streets

Spinoff

Arachnophilia

REVERSE HAREM

Warring Suns

SCI FI

The Essence of Esme

PARANORMAL

The Hunger of Thieves

Heart of The Reaper

Heart of the Reaper: Tales from the Underworld

Soul of The Reaper

Fate of The Reaper

Bury Me Alive

Lead Me Through The Fire

PSYCHOLOGICAL THRILLER

The Truth Enslaved

CONTEMPORARY

The Formation of Us

The Conception of Us

The Revelation of Us

The House of Eden (cowrite)

When the Bloom Burns (cowrite)

OMEGAVERSE

Gero

Bernhard

Severin

Dystopian/Post Apocalyptic

We Are the Fallen

MONSTER SHORT STORIES

Sinful Attraction

The Sky Below

Maeonia

Between Heaven and Earth

Fantasies Inflamed

Her 13th Hour

Ignus Fatuus

ANTHOLOGIES

Used and Bound

Captured by Darkness

Until the End

After the Rain

Into The Woods

A Foster Fling

Bound by Monsters

Once Upon a Nightmare

Monsters in Love: Lost in the Dark

Monsters in Love: Lost in the Forest

Monsters in Love: Monstrous Ever After

Monsters in Love: Lost in the Deeps

Monsters in Love: Aloha Nui Loa

Pollinators

The Red Key Club: Valentines Day Edition

The Red Key Club: Halloween Edition

Creepy Court

Crimson Vendetta

For the Love of Villains

SHARED WORLDS

Inferno World

Games of the Underworld

Rise of the Dreads

Monsters Ball

Rescue Me: A Hero Romance Collection

The Revelation of Us

Fabian Hernandez: The man who stole my first kiss.
My recently acquired brother-in-law.
From the moment he came into my life, he turned everything upside down.
There's a magnetism that keeps drawing us back together.
But we can't.
It isn't allowed.
It would bring shame.
It shouldn't have to be this hard, this complicated.
Maybe if I were someone else.
Someone without a controlling mother, a conservative culture.
A family and culture that sees this man as immediate family.
This is so difficult.
My hijab is getting too tight, everything around me is becoming too constricting.
Why must he drive me to the brink of madness with every touch, every kiss?
When things start to unravel, will I be strong enough to make the hardest decision of my life?

Courtesy Warning: This book may contain triggers for some. Triggers include but not limited to: violence, familial violence/abuse, subject matters that may be sensitive to some readers.

The Revelation of Us Snippet

Sakinah

Walking out through the front doors of the building, I'm trying my best to look down so I don't fall over the few steps down. Making it down alive, I almost released the breath I was holding only to run into something hard in front of me. But unlike last time, my books don't fall because the person is holding me by the arms with their strong arms.

"Oh, I'm so sorry! Man, why does this keep hap-" His cocky grin is the first thing I see and I already know who it belongs to. No one has a smile that can make panties melt like that on the science side of this damn campus. I know, I've looked...trying to find eye candy that could replace the image before me.

But no one does dreamy bad boy like Fabian Hernandez.

"What are you doing here Fabian?" Why my voice has so much attitude, I don't know. Just something about him that makes me put my guard up.

"Sakinah, why do you need to be like that? How about 'it's nice seeing you here or something?" He's kidding, right?

"I see you're here. What do you need?" Fabian laughs and my insides glow. It's a good thing my hijab is covering the flush that's probably showing on my skin. Those cute little crinkles by his eyes when he smiles like this make me want to drop my books and just climb him like a tree.

Instead, I'm frowning at him and waiting for him to stop laughing and attracting all the attention from the females nearby. Ugh. Why does he have to have this kind of energy? Why the hell do I feel like I want to claw all these girls' eyes out? This makes my mood worse.

"Sakinah, you're much more beautiful when you smile, you know that? What's up with the frown? Here, let me help you with those books." What the hell am I supposed to say to that? I want to be mad, but I can't. Yanking my books away from him, I continue like I didn't just act like a petulant brat.

"Fabian, is there a reason why you are here?"

"Well, since you asked so nicely... I just so happened to be in the neighborhood and who do I see? The girl I've been thinking about all day." This asshole probably tells all the girl's this. I can feel my face scrunching at the thought.

"We've already established this Fabian. I don't think this friendship thing is going to work out."

"Sakinah, Sakinah, Sakinah. Why must you give up on us so easily? Come on, we can hang like adults and not make a thing about it, right?" What is he trying to say? That I'm not an adult?

"Look here, old man. I don't know what you're insinuating with your comment."

"Fucking hell, Sakinah. I want to hang out with you. That's what I'm *insinuating*. Can't a guy try his damndest to get a pretty girl by his side?" I can feel the butterflies fluttering inside my stomach, but I can't let it show. How can he just stand there in his stupid boots, form fitted jeans and button down shirt looking like a delicious snack talking about me being pretty? Vero and her brother are two of a kind in their vintage rockabilly looks.

Judging by the lingering females around us, I'm not the only one who thinks this way.

"I'm sure you have plenty of women lined up for the chance. Why don't you choose from your usual pool of females hmm?" I'm fishing, I know it. He better not agree or else I will kick his ass until next Tuesday. I'm staring daggers at him just daring him to say something about another woman.

"Damn Sakinah. There isn't anyone else and even if there was, which there *isn't*, it's not their company I'm seeking alright. I'm here aren't I? Do you see anyone else but us? No." I'm scared. I'm scared to get my hopes up for a man like Fabian.

A man who could very well take my offered heart and stomp all over it if he finds something better along the way. My head starts to feel tight under my hijab and my body is starting to heat up from the embarrassment I feel for something that hasn't even happened yet.

That's the problem though, right? *Yet.*

Turning around without another word, I start walking towards the student parking lot. I need to get out of here. How does Fabian make my emotions feel like I'm freefalling from a rollercoaster just by talking to me?

I can hear his boots following me and I start walking faster. It's juvenile, I know. But I can't help the way this fucker makes me feel like punching him and kissing him all at once! Is this how little boys feel when they're young and on the playground around someone they like?

My car is coming in sight and I'm almost about to sprint but I can't because of the dress I'm in today. My hand is already reaching into my pocket and fishing out the keys but before I can stick it in the door, I'm spun around and trapped by a whole lot of Fabian. Holding my books closer to my chest like it's a shield, my head tilts up to look at him with fire. If I didn't have these books in my arms, I would slap him in the face ... again.

Fabian is thinking the same thing because with both arms on either side of me, leaning against my little sedan, he comes closer in with a smirk.

"Sakinah." My eyes narrow.

"Fabian."

"Why are you being like this?"

"Like what?" Ugh, why *am* I like this?

"You should want to be around me. We're family after all."

"Yeah well, family shouldn't be asking each other out on dates then."

"Sakinah, go out with me. You might enjoy it more than you think...if you'd just let yourself."

"I'm busy that day." His laugh booms across the parking lot making even more girls stop. He needs to quit this shit. It's pissing me off.

"I haven't even decided on the date yet!"

"You don't have to. I'm busy."

Quicker than I can react, Fabian grabs my textbooks and puts them on top of the roof of my car right behind me, never letting me out of the cage of his arms.

"Sakinah."

"Fabian."

I'm about to open my mouth to tell him to fuck off somewhere else when his lips crash on mine again. This man...

This man's lips are so damn soft as he uses them expertly against mine and I can't help but fall prey to his wicked ways...

My god, Fabian is sin on a stick and I don't know how my arms ended up winding around his shoulders, pulling him into me even more. When he groans into my mouth as my breasts press against his chest, the spell of the moment gets broken. I nip his lip and push him as hard as my body will allow me.

Like the coward I am once more, I jump and grab my books before getting into the car and slamming the door shut. Letting out a long breath, I close my eyes but not before I lock the damn doors.

A thump startles me and has me looking out the side window to see Fabian rubbing his forehead on my car. This shouldn't look as endearing as it does. What is wrong with him? Why is he like this? His voice floats into the car like a muffle.

"Sakinah, this isn't over." He straightens up and bores his eyes into mine, full of promises that make my nipples tighten. His intensity scares me. I don't know how to handle everything that is Fabian Hernandez, not like this. I don't know what I'm feeling, everything is so confusing. Even being the most rebellious sister didn't prepare me for a force of nature like him.

www.ingramcontent.com/pod-product-compliance
Lightning Source LLC
Chambersburg PA
CBHW071415200726
48294CB00002B/400
* 9 7 8 1 9 6 2 4 0 3 0 6 1 *